STEAMY SHORTS 2

A Collection of Steampunk, Science Fiction
and other Erotic Short Stories

By
Jean Ecrivain

Copyright & Legal

© 2015, All rights reserved
Cover designed by Lisa Gravelle-Ford,
http://www.dragonportraits.com
© 2014 used with permission

ISBN: 978-1506136646

THIS IS A WORK OF FICTION. All characters, events, and locations are the product of the writer's imagination. Any resemblance to any person living or dead or any location or other is purely coincidence. And completely unbelievable.
The activities depicted in this book are intended for the entertainment of adults. If you are below the age of majority in your jurisdiction, PLEASE STOP READING. The author and/or publisher and/or bookseller is not responsible for the purchase or use of this book in jurisdictions where depiction of adult relationship activities is forbidden. If you are in such a jurisdiction, PLEASE STOP READING. The activities depicted in this book may or may not be harmful, dangerous, or even impossible. In any case, they should not be attempted in real life. In real life always practice safe, sane, and consensual sex.

R20150204.092800

For my readers;
you inspire me,
motivate me,
and
give me reason to write

Hope you all like it.

Other Books by Jean Ecrivain

On Kindle:
A Taste for the Night Series
A Taste for the Night Book 1 Arrival
A Taste for the Night Book 2 Settling In

Chasing Fae Romance Series
Book 1 Well Met in Forest Light
Book 2 Well Met in Castle Light

Steamy Shorts
Steamy Shorts 1
Steamy Shorts 2
Steamy Shorts 3 (due February/March 2015)

In Print:
A Taste for the Night Series
A Taste for the Night Book 2 Settling In
(includes Bonus of Book 1)

Chasing Fae Romance Series
Book 1 Well Met in Forest Light
Book 2 Well Met in Castle Light

Steamy Shorts
Steamy Shorts 1
Steamy Shorts 2
Steamy Shorts 3 (due February/March 2015)

Table of Contents

INTRODUCTION	**1**
A NOTE FROM THE AUTHOR	1
1. THE BONNY BLACK HARE	**3**
PREFACE	3
THE BONNY BLACK HARE	7
2. THE SEX JIN	**29**
PREFACE	29
THE SEX JIN	31
3. CYBER SEXED	**55**
PREFACE	55
CYBER SEXED	57
4. SWORDS AND SEXERY	**75**
PREFACE	75
SWORDS AND SEXERY	79
5. WELL MET IN THE FOREST	**97**
PREFACE	97
WELL MET IN THE FOREST	101
NOTES FROM THE AUTHOR	**115**
A NOTE FROM THE AUTHOR	115
ABOUT THE AUTHOR	117
OTHER BOOKS BY JEAN ECRIVAIN	**119**
SAMPLES	**120**
A TASTE FOR THE NIGHT BOOK 1 ARRIVAL	121
A TASTE FOR THE NIGHT BOOK 2 SETTLING IN	129
CHASING FAE ROMANCE BOOK 1 WELL MET IN FOREST LIGHT	141

| Chasing Fae Romance Book 2 Well Met in Castle Light | 149 |
| The Steamy Shorts series | 167 |

Introduction

Welcome to the second book in my Steamy Shorts series.

There are two questions that every writer gets. And every writer dreads. The first is, "How do you get your ideas?" And the second is, "How do you write a book?"

The reason every writer dreads the first is that the answer is just too simple to satisfy the querist. Ideas are everywhere. Literally. And the more you write the more ideas for books you get. One leads inevitably to the other. Sun following shower. In fact, there are far too many ideas to ever write all the books you might wish to. The problem, in fact, is to pare down those ideas to just those that are worthy of becoming a book.

The reason every writer dreads the second question, is that the answer is just too complex to avoid overwhelming the querist. For non-fiction there is a single right answer. But for fiction, there are more answers than there are successful writers. Everyone works slightly differently and every book is written slightly differently. Part of the apprenticeship of a writer is to determine the method that works best for them. And the apprenticeship never stops.

In my case, I start by writing an idea into a single sentence (if I can) and a single paragraph if there's just too much to fit into a dozen words. That helps me make sure that a week from now, I won't forget that wonderful idea that woke me up in the middle of the night demanding to be written RIGHT NOW. I then write the core of the idea as a short story. That tells me if I've really got a story or not and if the writing will be more work than pleasure. If it passes that test, then I'll design a plot. That tells me if there's enough in the story to fill a whole book (or series) and gives me the framework for the book. Then, and only then, I go on to write the book, usually using the short story as the first chapter. After all, time is money and I only have a limited amount of time available. Besides, I have to like the short story to write it as a novel!

As you can guess, I tend to have a large backlog of stories. Some that haven't made the cut. Some that haven't passed the plot stage. Some that I'm just not

Chapter 1 Underhill

going to get to. And some that I just haven't finished yet.

I have also written short stories for as long as I can remember. Whatever my interests, I'm sure I have a short story somewhere that reflects it. But I really haven't had anywhere to use them before now. So for many years, I was a writer without readers.

In short, I have a backlog of short stories filling up my computer disk with nowhere to use them.

At the same time, I've discovered that writing full-length novels (and series) is a long-winded process. Although I was able to release four novels in a little over a year, there's actually a long period between each book. And that time is getting longer. I'm estimating that my next book is at least six months away.

Unfortunately, I rely on my books to pay rent, bills and put food on my table. So the longer between books, the more I have to charge to recoup my investment of time, energy and yes, money. It doesn't take long before the cost of my books exceeds what the market is willing to pay.

Six months is too long between books for a new writer like myself. I wanted (and needed) to publish books more frequently with no more than two months between each book. All while giving myself enough time to write my next full length novel.

But how?

Thus this series was born.

In this series, you'll find everything I'm interested in. From space opera to steampunk, from urban fantasy to historical romance. The only unifying thread is that the characters love sex in all its myriad forms. And they enjoy being characters in an Erotic novel.

I hope you'll enjoy reading about them as much as I enjoy writing about them. And if we each have half as much fun as they have living their Erotica stories, then we should both be very satisfied.

By the way, if there is a particular story you would like to see as a book, or a particular scene you would like portrayed in a future short story, please let

Chapter 1 Underhill

me know. You can contact me via Facebook at https://www.facebook.com/jean.ecrivain or send me an email at jeanecrivain@gmail.com .

Jean E.
Ontario, Canada

A note from the author

Most writers enjoy spreading their wings. Most writers also depend on their readers for inspiration. This book is an extreme example of those two characteristics.

Because these are short stories, I can take chances. I can write stories that go beyond my rather perverted (and. so I'm learning, rather limited) interests and fantasies.

But to do that I need your help.

If there is anything you would like me to write about – situation, theme, sex act, characters – anything at all, please ask. That's all it will take.

You can contact me (and follow me) through either my Facebook page which can be found at https://www.facebook.com/jean.ecrivain or also through my Amazon authors page which can be found at http://www.amazon.com/author/jeanecrivain or via good old email at jeanecrivain@gmail.com. Of course, you can also find me on one of the many Facebook groups I hang out in. I do respond to everyone and I really do want your opinions. So come along and say hello.

Jean E.

Ontario, Canada

1. The Bonny Black Hare

Preface

Word play, especially erotic word play, has been an element of poetry and song for as long as music has been sung. My inspiration for this story was a combination of several influences from music to stories.

I wanted to include in the collection somewhere at least one story involving the were-. Were-wolves are extremely popular in erotic fiction at the moment. So I wanted to try my hand at writing one. But of course, a simple boy meets girl, boy turns out to be an animal just wasn't enough for me. After all that's just real life, isn't it? My books are a way to explore what isn't real (and in many cases not even possible). I needed something a little different for my story. And I'm more of a 'girl as animal, boy as prey' type of girl.

I also wanted to explore a little furry-play. Furries, for those of you unfamiliar with the scene, are humanized animals common in Japanese anime and several underground comics. Most of the comics have a definite adult bent to them. The movement has grown to include a large contingent of fans who dress up in costume as animals. Whenever you bring together a number of hard-partying fans with a common interest, you inevitably have a kink developing around the interest. And so it is with Furries.

The third element is somewhat personal. I have a furry little bunny that has invaded my front yard. He or she has taken to living in the bushes that surround my home. We often are greeted by our fearless little invader as we leave our home. He/she tends to sit there and wait for us to go by. Our own little greeter. So far my garden has been avoided by the little beastie. There's enough long grass to keep him/her well-fed. So my feelings about this cutie may change if he/she changes his/her feeding habits.

Finally, as I've mentioned elsewhere, my taste in music is quite wide. Amongst my musical interests are traditional music and the folk-rock movement (and heavy rock, heavy metal, pirate metal, and classical music and … you get the picture). I'm a little eccentric in my tastes. The Bonny Black Hare is a traditional tune sung by both Fairport Convention and Steeleye Span (amongst others). While both versions are very different, they both are part of my writing playlist. And the song

Story 1 The Bonny Black Hare

has been a part of my want-to-write list for as long as I can remember.

While I didn't quite get my Furry story, mix the four elements together and you end up with this story.

I hope you enjoy it and I will do a Furry story for a future collection. Promise.

The Bonny Black Hare

It was amazing that he saw the cabin door at all, hidden as it was in the mound of grass, earth, and roots. The door seemed at first glance to grow right out of the natural hillock that had erupted between the roots of the massive oak. But as he looked closer, he realized that the hillock was really a sod house. It had been there so long that the grass roof had grown to flow down the wall so that the house now resembled a natural hill. An oak tree had taken root at the edge of the house long ago. Over the ages, the tree had grown and it now dwarfed the house that had once sheltered it. If the black hare he had been chasing hadn't run into the bushes under the window, he would never have seen the cottage.

Sir Hugh closed his eyes in relief and rested his forehead for a moment on the cold steel barrel of his hunting rifle. His long red hair hung down over the fancy Kentucky long rifle styled flintlock. Twigs and leaves tumbled out of his hair to float or drop into the duff on the forest floor. His shoulders relaxed and the stress scraped off his back to join the black mud at his feet. With a sigh, he lifted his head from its resting place and he stumbled to the door. The drum beat of his fist rumbled through the hillock and echoed out of the tiny windows that peaked from the cob.

"Please, miss. The lord of these lands, your lord, Sir Hugh seeks entrance. I wandered apart from my hunting party and have become lost. I seek shelter for the night. You have no reason to worry. I will not harm you or any within. Open and give me entrance."

The eyes that peaked around the partially opened door were young. Blue irises peaked around a large black pupil. Her upper lip trembled and her fingers clutched at the edge of the door. Black locks hung down almost to her waist. Her dress may have once been black but had now faded to brown. A grey apron hung at her waist.

From what Sir Hugh could see, the girl was young. Just a few years younger than Sir Hugh's own 23 summers. However, a peasant's life was hard and a woodsman's even harder. It aged a person quickly. Sir Hugh knew she could have been anywhere from thirteen to her early twenties. Peasant women married at fifteen and were burned up by thirty. Even if she had stood properly before him, he would be hard put to judge. And

Story 1 The Bonny Black Hare

with her hiding most of her form behind the door, he had little to base a guess on.

"Come now, girl. I give you my word, as your sworn lord, and as a knight and gentleman. You will come to no harm at my hands. I am lost and in need of shelter for the night. In the morning, I will be off again. I have my own provisions so I will not even ask to be fed. Nor will I disturb you from your own bed. A place by the fire, a roof over my head, and walls to save me from the wolves. That is all I ask."

At the mention of wolves, the girl jumped and scanned the forest surrounding the tiny house. Finding nothing, she inspected the hunter with fear written on every bone and muscle. With a shake, she seemed to conclude that hospitality outweighed caution. Throwing open the door, she stepped to the side and beckoned him within. She said nothing as she bolted the door behind him.

"Thank you, mistress. My name is Hugh. I was hunting a huge black hare and it led me a merry chase. Unfortunately, I wandered off the path and became lost. I am thankful for the shelter."

"Hugh. A strong name. A hunter's name. I am called Andred. If you come in peace then be welcome to my home. Come sit by the fire. I have some stew heating. It's not much but it's warm and filling. And there's plenty. I'll get you a bowl and some bread."

Hugh stumbled into the darkened room. A fire blazed in what would have been called the far corner, if a round house could be said to have corners. A small kitchen preparation area spread out from one side of the massive stone fireplace and a couch was built into the wall on the other side. Several large chairs and small tables were arranged in front of the fire. Colorful pillows and rugs covered every flat surface. Hugh could see a doorway leading to a bedroom behind the fireplace. A hallway led off from the wall opposite the fireplace.

"Your clothes are wet and you'll freeze if you stay that way. Strip yourself down. Hang your coat and shoes beside the fire to dry. There's a wrap on the chair for modesty's sake. Then sit yourself in a chair and I'll bring the food. Food and warmth, and getting out of those wet clothes. That's what ye need."

"I have my own provisions, and I don't want to dishonor you in your own home. What would your

Story 1 The Bonny Black Hare

husband say if he came home to find a naked man warming himself by your fire?"

"Don't be ten times a fool. I'll not have you pulling out that foul stuff you laughingly call trail food. Not in my home, I won't. And I'm old enough to have seen what a man has between his legs and more of them than you, I daresay. As for a husband, if I had one and I don't, he'd trust me to honor the marriage bed in my own way or he'd be gone sooner than a flea from a hairless cat. Strip. Hang. Sit. I'll get the bread and bowl. And I'll be thanking you to stand on the hearth when you strip. It can be easily washed, the rugs can't. Use the ash bucket to wring your cloak."

Hugh pulled his cloak off and wrung it out into the ask bucket. He hung the sodden mass on a peg below the mantle. His boots were next. He poured out the water from them while his socks squished on the hot stones of the hearth. The soggy leathers were stored beneath his cloak. His socks were next onto a peg, after they had been wrung out tightly into the bucket that was now almost full of water and ash.

Hugh stood before the fire debating on whether to argue further with the young woman. But as the fire warmed his body, the cold clamminess of his shirt and pants decided the matter for him. With a shiver, he pulled the wet shirt over his head and hung it on a peg. Hugh rubbed briskly at his strong, hard-muscled torso and upper arms, trying desperately to rub the heat from the fire into cold skin. The exercise gave him good excuse to delay removing his last testament to modesty and he dragged it out as long as he could.

A shiver twisted and turned his spine. With a glance at Andred, Hugh peeled off his pants, stripping them down his damp legs. Soon he stood nude and shivering before the fire. His hands slipped down his groin and he rubbed quickly trying to drive heat back into his cock and balls. Even shrunken from the cold, his cock was longer and thicker than most. And as his hands flew over his groin and thighs, driving blood and heat back into his extremities, the long rod grew longer and thicker.

As Andred stood at the counter preparing the bread, she fought the urge to turn and stare. Instead, she stole little glances at Hugh's reflection in the window. When he revealed his manhood, she let out a gasp of surprise which she covered by dropping a knife. It clattered against the counter and the pots of butter. She shook herself and forced herself to concentrate on the bread and the bowls. She could feel her face growing warm and a slickness building between her legs. Her legs shifted under her skirt and her nipples burned.

She delayed as long as she could, but soon Andred had no choice but to turn and fill the bowls with the warm stew. She carefully kept her eyes averted from Hugh and his movements. Instead, she moved to the large kettle that stood over the fire and ladled large portions of stew over the bread that sat in the bowls. Hugh smiled as he noticed her efforts to avoid embarrassing him. He wrapped a blanket around his shoulders and legs and plopped down into one of the chairs.

"There is no meat in the stew, I'm afraid. But you'll find there's good carrots and potatoes, leaks and turnips, and pumpkin and chick peas aplenty. It's hot and tasty and should fill the space between your ribs, sir knight."

"Forgive me, mistress. Let me add my dried meat. I won't feel as if I'm stealing food from someone who can ill afford to spare any."

"No. Keep that foul stuff in your pack and out of my food. There's more than enough stew. The forest has plenty of food for those who know it well. If you wish seconds or even thirds, you must serve yourself. There's only a few more slices of bread, but that's because I only bake enough for myself and it would take too much time to bake more."

Hugh sat back in the chair and wrapped his hands around the proffered bowl. He shoveled a spoonful of the stew into his mouth and stared at it in surprise. It was good. Spicy and thick, even a single mouthful warmed him to the bones. He could feel the heat spreading down his chest and arms and rolling through his groin. He shoveled the food into his mouth and watched Andred as she sat in the other chair delicately nibbling on her meal.

Andred was tiny for a woman surviving on her own in the forest. She was trim but softly curved and almost ten inches shorter than Hugh's six-foot frame. Her soft breasts were small and obviously unsupported beneath the black peasant blouse. Hugh could clearly see the hard, pointed tips poking through the thin material. Her hair was long and black. It cascaded down her back, though it spread into a shawl while she was seated. Her nose was small and wiggled while she sipped from the stew. Her jaw was bouncing like a beaver on a tree as she nibbled on the vegetable pieces.

As Hugh spooned the stew into his mouth, he could feel his strength returning and the heat building in his groin. He could feel his cock growing harder as he watched Andred's tits shivering as she nibbled her supper. To take his mind off her body, he began to talk about his hunting trip. How he had spotted a large black hare in the hedgerows. How his first shot had missed and he had chased it into the forest lest he leave a wounded animal to die in pain. The forest that he had been forbidden to enter because it was so dangerous. How he had chased that hare through the forest, leaving his entourage to follow as best they could. How the hare had teased him, leading him through bramble thickets and muddy streams. Most of which he had fallen into. How he had tripped over a branch and tumbled down a hill. How he had become lost and eventually ended up here.

As entertainment, he found his tale worked well, and Andred was laughing wildly at his misadventures by the time he finished. But as a method of taking his mind off his companion, it failed miserably. Andred's tits shook wildly as she laughed and her eyes glistened. Her nipples were hard buds pointing through her top. By the time he shoveled the last of the vegetables into his mouth, his cock was so swollen that it hurt. His need had turned to a sour taste in the back of his throat and it hurt to breath. As he sat there watching her for a few minutes more, his breath was labored and he whined softly.

"If you wish more, ye'll have to fetch it yourself. I'll serve you once for your sake. But twice only to pleasure me."

Hugh could feel his face heating and he cursed his fair skin. Sheepishly, he gathered his blanket around him and stood to ladle more stew into his bowl. He reached out and lifted the big ladle from the mantle. That was when he realized his other hand could either hold the blanket tight to his body or extend so the bowl could be filled. He stood for a moment gathering his thoughts and wondering how to get out of this mire. With a sigh, he clamped the blanket between his elbows and his sides and extended both arms. The blanket slid open displaying a length of thigh and groin, but fortunately for his modesty's sake and to Andred's disappointment, his raging hardon was still hidden in the folds of wool. Andred stared at his contortions, her teeth chewing on her lower lip. Her breath came in great gulps and she licked her suddenly dry lips.

Story 1 The Bonny Black Hare

Hugh stretched his arms out and fought to pour stew into his bowl without offending his hostess. He filled the bowl and managed to turn to go back to his chair to Andred's obvious disappointment. That was when he stepped on the trailing material of the blanket. With a pop, the blanket pulled from under his clamped elbows and tumbled to the floor.

Hugh stood trembling on the hearth, one hand holding a full bowl of stew and the other the large iron ladle. His nipples were hard buds on the crisp plates of his chest. His stomach was a patchwork of muscles and his thick cock stood proudly from his body surrounded by a forest of red hair. Andred leaned forward in her chair. Her tongue slid over suddenly dry lips. She wheezed as she sucked air into her lungs. Her hands slipped to her thighs and squeezed. Her eyes flicked over his body, lingering on the hot meat that stood out from between his mighty thighs and then flickering up to stare in his eyes and then back again. She moaned quietly and then levered herself up to a standing position.

Andred gently took the bowl and ladle from Hugh's trembling hands. She hung the ladle back on the mantle and then placed the bowl gently on the table. Her hands slid over his shoulders and then down his chest. Her fingers flicked against his hard nipples bringing a moan to his lips.

"I think you need something to eat other than vegetable stew. And we both have other hungers that need to be fed. At least judging by that growth between your legs. Come with me."

Andred's hands slid over Hugh's strong chest and down his stomach. Her fingers slipped around his rod and she squeezed tightly. With a coquettish smile, she led him toward the bedroom and the built-in overstuffed canopy bed. One hand pulled on his hard cock as he trailed behind. The other trailed over his groin and balls leaving sparkling firefly tracks on his skin.

Hugh was writhing and groaning by the time the stood before the large, overstuffed bed. The reds, and whites, and yellows, and blues of the thick coverlet echoed off his eyeballs in swirls of color. They bounced off the fog of desire that left his stomach queasy and his lower body quaking. When Andred stood on tiptoe and tipped up her mouth to him, he could think of nothing but bringing his own mouth down on those oh-so red lips. His body followed his desires and he soon became

Story 1 The Bonny Black Hare

lost in the battle between their tongues. Each fought for dominance. Each fought for entrance. Each fought in a battle where there was no loser, drawing desire from the other. Hugh could feel his cock harden even more until it was an aching band of steel that ripped out his groin with every tortuous bounce.

Andred slid her hands up Hugh's body, to caress his chest and back. Her hard nipples burned against his chest through the barrier of her top. Her hands slipped over his back, thrilling to the feel of soft skin over hard muscle. The feel of bone and gristle and muscle burned up her arms and over her chest.

Hugh fought to keep his hands off her for as long as he could. Honor fought with desire over physical need and lost. With a groan of overwhelming need, he seized her in his strong arms. He could feel her heat on his hands through the thin cloth of her blouse. The soft cushions of her breasts burned into his chest. Overwhelmed with his own need and her desire, he crushed her tiny body into his with a moan.

Andred sighed as she felt Hugh's strong arms crushing her. Her breasts were squeezed into flat ovals, her nipples burning into his chest. She could feel the heat from his hard cock poking her in the stomach. She could feel his back clenching under her hands. She could feel his hot hands slipping down her back and clutching her round ass. She could feel the hot invading wetness of his tongue tickling over her lips and teeth, fighting for entrance, seeking to dance again and again with her tongue.

His hands pulling on her top, dragging it up her sides brought a moan rumbling deep in her stomach. The soft material slid along her sensitive skin. Sparks of fire tumbled up her back in the wake of the cloth. Her skirts followed quickly after to lie in a heap at her feet. She shivered for a moment as the cold air tumbled over her bare skin but his hands quickly returned to hold her, bathing her in heat and desire. Her own hands flew over his back and sides. She slid them up his chest, loving the feel of muscle and skin beneath her palms. Andred clutched Hugh's shoulders and pulled herself up into his kiss.

Their tongues danced as each explored the other's mouth. Tickling at the heat and wetness. Leaving trails of fire and desire on the flesh of lips and gums and roof. Andred could feel the soft tip of Hugh's cock pressing against her stomach, knocking at the door as he flexed in need, seeking entrance to her nest below.

Story 1 The Bonny Black Hare

Andred ground her hips against Hugh, giggling as his cock jumped and he groaned. The giggles turned to a moan as she fed harder on his questing tongue and his hands clutched tighter on her ass.

Andred pushed on his chest forcing Hugh away. Their lips stuck to each other until the very end. Until with a mutual sigh, they both released their hold. Andred caressed his cheek and kissed him lightly on the chin. She bent forward, her lips and tongue leaving a trail down his body. It started just beneath his lips and travelled backwards along his strong jaw. Then down over the slight scratchiness of his neck. His shoulders were next as she got lost amongst the hills and valleys that led downwards to his chest. Her mouth stalled in its trek for a moment, sucking on his hard nipples. Her tongue flicked over and around the hard buds. Her teeth seized them in their turn and dragged them away his chest, only to release them and then follow up with an apologizing kiss and lick. And still her lips and tongue slid further down. A trail of fire and ice travelling down his body. Down to the soft patch of fur below the stomach.

Andred's hands gripped Hugh's firm ass as her tongue explored the forest above his prick. Her tongue twisted in the hairs, sending bolts of sensation exploding through his groin and up his spine. Hugh was shaking now, his hands gripping her head, holding himself in position. Maintaining control by only the barest of threads.

Her mouth slid around his hardness, chewing on the pulsing length of flesh. Her tongue flicked over the soft skin as she chewed her way to the soft purple head. Her tongue flicked around the soft skin beneath the glans. She twisted and twirled her tongue and then flicked out over the soft spongy mushroom head. Andred could feel Hugh's groan vibrating through his hard rod. She smiled to herself as she opened her mouth wide and swallowed his length.

Andred forced the long fleshy rod past her lips and over her tongue. When she felt it striking her throat she paused a moment to allow her throat to adjust. Then slowly she forced it past her uvula and down the long shaft of her gullet. She hummed sending vibrations trilling up his groin. She could feel Hugh spasm as he reacted to her song. Slowly she pulled back, her tongue trailing on the soft flesh as she withdrew. Then slowly she worked her way down the shaft, tasting and sucking on the hard rod until her nose was buried in the forest that surrounded his cock. Hugh was groaning loudly and she smiled as she felt his throbbing response.

Story 1 The Bonny Black Hare

Once again, her head bobbed slipping the rod out of her mouth then plunging along its length. Faster and faster, she slid along his prick, until her head was pounding against his flesh, and Hugh could only stand and quiver under the onslaught. His legs shook and his hips jerked uncontrollably.

With a scream, Hugh erupted in Andred's mouth. Thick white cream sprayed out of his hard rod and splashed against the back of her throat. Andred could taste its saltiness and she gulped as she fought to swallow the waves of hot liquid. Despite her best efforts, it filled her mouth and pushed its way over her teeth and gums. It bubbled out of her lips around his hard cock, leaving trails of white cream dripping down her chin.

Andred slid up his body until she stood in front of Hugh. She stared deep into his eyes as she licked her lips. With a single finger, she mopped up his juices where they had dribbled down her chin. Her finger slid between her red lips and her tongue rolled around the digit. Andred hummed as she sucked at the salty liquid. She smiled predatorily at Hugh.

"Now it's my turn, good Sir Hugh."

Andred seized Hugh by his long prick and dragged him with her to the bed. Her back made a muffled slapping sound against the thick comforters. Air whooshed from her lungs. Hugh stared at her for a moment, overwhelmed by her beauty. With an inarticulate cry, he jumped onto the bed beside her. His mouth found hers in a paroxysm of desire. His lips crushed against her red lips. Her tongue fought its way past the fleshy boundary and slid into his mouth. His tongue fought a losing battle slapping and sliding over hers, driving back against the intruder.

As they broke apart to drag deep breaths, Hugh slid down Andred's body. His lips left a trail of soft kisses, down her neck, across her shoulders and down to her breast. His tongue trailed around her soft mound until it tripped across the hard nubbin that crowned the whiteness. His mouth slipped over the brown crinkled flesh and he sucked on the swollen nob. His tongue flicked over her nipple as he drew it deep into his mouth.

Onwards he continued to kiss, sliding over her soft mounded tummy and down over her mound. His tongue flicked around the bush of red hair that hid her lips, sliding along the fold of skin between leg and groin. He played in the woodlands, twisting and twirling the long crinkled hairs. Andred moaned, her hips bouncing upwards, driving Hugh's mouth closer to her steadily leaking slit.

Sir Hugh's tongue flicked along Andred's slit, licking over the outer lips, his teeth chewing gently on the soft flesh. Andred's breath was coming quickly now in quick, jagged gasps. Her hips shook and her cunt spasmed in need driving desire upwards over her stomach and tightening her soft breasts and nipples.

Andred screamed as Hugh's tongue fluttered along her slit and over the hard nob of her clit. His teeth and lips nipped at her soft folds and his tongue pulled at her lips. His tongue plucked at her hood and the hard red shaft within. Waves of sensation rolled up her tummy and exploded behind her eyes.

Hugh's mouth never left her body as he slid up her. He stared deep into her eyes as his hard shaft played amongst the folds that guarded her inner cavern. His hard shaft slid through the liquid lips and squeezed into her. Andred's head rolled as she felt his hardness splitting her and driving deep into her insides. Her breathing grew frantic as he pushed into her. Her eyes rolled backward as he pounded the hard rod into her soft caverns.

Andred could feel the veins that lined Hugh's hard shaft rubbing along her lips. She could feel his thickness stretching and filling her. The rubbing and pounding on her clit sent waves of need exploding up her spine.

Hugh and Andred screamed together as Hugh erupted in a boiling burst of semen. Andred bit her lip as she felt her own release clutching at her pussy and turning it into a seething whirlwind of sensations. She could feel his body twist between her legs as his climax rolled up his spine.

***

Hugh threw his pack over his shoulder. He gently closed the cottage door and turned to look at the sun-dappled clearing. With a shake of his head, he slowly moved off across the bare patch. As he reached the woods, he turned and glanced at the cottage for one last time. He thought for a moment that he saw Andred at the window. But he shook his head as he realized that she had probably forgotten him as soon as he left the cottage. It wasn't as though they could have a life together. With a sigh, he turned reluctantly off and trudged through the gloom of the forest.

The bushes below the window shook for a moment. A big black hare stuck her nose between the bushes. Her coat was black once but now was faded to brown and her belly was grey. She sat for a moment, her head the only visible indication of its presence. Her nose bounced in eagerness as she scented the air. As a crash came from the woods across the clearing, her head came up and she stared at the green leaves that Hugh had knocked askew. She took a deep breath and blew it out with a whistle. With a thump of her powerful legs, she bounded out of the covering of foliage. For a moment, she sat enjoying the sun that baked the clearing and listening to the fading crunches and crashes. Then she bounded quickly into the forest in pursuit of the slowly retreating noise, her fluffy white tail flipping in the wind and her grey belly visible for all to see.

2. The Sex Jin

Preface

In Well Met in Castle Light, I introduced a jewel merchant called Hassan. He was a minor character but he had a major part to play in the full story. He lasted less than a chapter and is probably never going to reappear.

The problem was that he was a wonderful character. A bit of a rogue with an eye for the ladies and a wife who was a renowned swordsmistress. With a temper and a jealous streak. In short, the type of guy that makes female writers cream their pants. (Don't get any ideas Toy).

Did I mention that he was also a Jinn?

I decided I wanted to write a story involving both him and his wife to include in this series. He was just too delicious a character to let disappear. As I was trying to think of a story to include him, I came up with a story for his wife (Swords & Sexery) and this one.

Which didn't help with coming up for a story for him but gave me two good stories for this collection.

The funny thing is that as I was fighting with this story, I realized that it was really a novella rather than a short story. So you may see this as the first chapter of a standalone novel at some time in the future. We shall see.

I hope you enjoy reading this as much as I enjoyed writing it.

The Sex Jin

Charlie picked up the old brass bottle. It was definitely brass from its wide base to the stopper stuck firmly in its thin throat. And it was almost certainly old. He held it in both hands marveling at its warmth and admiring the way the dappled light brought out the strange lettering that covered the bottle.

Charlie blinked as his eyes adapted to looking up, the glare bouncing off his thick glasses. The thrift shop was old and dingy. He preferred old and dingy. It matched his mood. The city was old and dingy. The street was old and dingy. School was old and dingy. Life was old and dingy. He was old and dingy. Why shouldn't the thrift shop be old and dingy? He liked old and dingy.

Charlie jumped as three high-school students banged through the door and into the shop. Their music blared throughout the store boosting the volume of the store's own radio, which was playing the same rock tune. They stopped for a moment to flirt with the young man behind the psychedelic counter as they made for the brightly lit, multicolored clothing stacks at the back of the store. Their laughter and excitement jangled on his nerves.

Charlie shuddered and tried to block the noise assaulting his ears. But it wasn't long before he gave it up as a lost cause. With a grimace at the teenaged girls, he broke off his explorations and headed to the counter. Charlie took his find directly to the young man who cowered behind the counter. The two bucks bounced off the cash register and he almost ran out the store. Past the drunk asleep in the doorway, into the stinking crowd, across the street and onto the bus. He didn't expect to find a seat on the bus and he wasn't disappointed or surprised at the crowd packing the stinking public transit vehicle. He stood in the crowded bus, one hand clutching his find, the other clutching the sticky leather strap while he tried to let his legs absorb the jerking motion of the rush-hour bus.

Charlie stuck the key into the door of his apartment and tried to ignore the smell from the hall. There were only two lights out this time, he thought, place must be renovating. He blinked as the overhead lights flickered on in response to his fist slamming into the switch by the door. Charlie wandered over to the bookshelf opposite the mattress that was his bed and placed the bottle on one of the less crowded shelves. One more knickknack for his student digs. Not much but hey, what do you expect on a University student's income? Especially a history major. Especially one that

Story 2 The Sex Jin

even the local fast food holes had blacklisted from employment.

The bottle kept drawing his gaze as he fiddled about in the kitchen. Yesterday's instant mac'n'cheese and hamburger piled on his cleanest dirty plate was tossed in the old microwave for two minutes. While he waited, Charlie rinsed a fork under the tap and then dumped it on the now-hot plate. He carried the whole mess into the living room and the rickety chair that was his only concession to proper furniture.

Charlie tried to watch the old black and white television in the corner. But his eyes kept sliding to the brass bottle on his shelf. It took only five minutes and a half dozen forkfuls until he got up, reached over to put the half-eaten plate of macaroni on the last clear spot on the kitchen counter, and then walked the ten feet to turn the flickering screen off. On the way back to the chair, he grabbed the bottle and a dust rag and cleaner from the shelf.

Charlie rubbed the moistened rag over the bottle, covering the entire surface in a continuous swipe. The rag turned black from the accumulated grime of what must have been centuries. Charlie peered at the marks dug deep into the brass. They appeared to be some form of Aramaic to Charlie's academic eyes. But the words seemed to keep shifting and he removed his glasses and rubbed at his eyes after only a few moments of trying to read the ancient script.

Charlie rubbed for a moment at a particularly blackened piece of brass. But the letters still jumped about beneath his eyes. They seemed to form a word but then they shifted and formed another. Then they were a meaningless jumble of symbols and words. Charlie blinked and shook his head.

The neck was particularly dirty, so Charlie anchored the bottle against his crotch. He wet the rag once again and began to rub the rag up and down the neck. He giggled to himself at the symbolism of his hand stripping up and down the neck of the bottle. Too bad, he wasn't that big in real life. The women would be all over him then. Charlie's smile faded as his mind slipped over the lack of companionship in his life. Women just didn't know what they wanted, he thought to himself. They weren't interested in nice guys like him. They only wanted the bad boys. And the crooks flashing their money and BMWs all over the place.

Story 2 The Sex Jin

Charlie sighed, and his hand slipped off the neck of the bottle. He peered at the writing in wonder. As soon as he had stopped rubbing, the writing had begun to glow. Now it burned in words of fire against the brass. Charlie gulped as the bottle began to vibrate against his crotch. His cock jumped and hardened in response to the vibrations trilling through his groin.

Charlie rubbed at his crotch where the bottle rubbed against his hardness. The bottle was bouncing on his groin, pounding the bent member into his flesh. It twirled around in his hands. The flaming words seemed to lift off the brass and hang in the air. Charlie jumped as the stopper flew off, hitting the opposite wall and bouncing back to ricochet off his arm and into the remains of his meal.

Pink and grey smoke flowed from the neck of the bottle. It eddied and swirled in a cloud of pinks and greys shot through with fire. It crawled down his leg, across the floor, and broke against the wall. It bubbled up along the wall in long fingers of pink and streaks of grey.

Charlie's scream as the cloud burst into a shower of bright light was echoed by the scream of the young lady who appeared with her back against the wall. Charlie blinked frantically against the bright afterimages, trying not to lose sight of the beautiful nude female who stood before him.

"Bugger me with the bloody seven hells. God damn it. No sooner do I get in the bath then someone rubs the damn lamp. Happens every fuckin' time. Fuck me. This better be an important wish or I swear ..."

Charlie gaped at the young, nude woman who stood before him, her red hair dripping on his floor. Her brown nipples peaked from behind a white froth. Soap bubbles lounged along her soft breasts and slid slowly lower revealing glimpses of warm flesh. Water dripped down between her breasts, over her soft round tummy, and down her mound. A large bubble of soap slid down her dark red pubic fleece to hide the pink slit that was just visible beneath. She was easily the most beautiful woman he had ever seen. Even if she was the first nude woman he had actually seen in the flesh. Charlie still knew she was the most beautiful woman he had ever seen, even in his dreams.

"What are you staring at? Got your fill of gawking? Now, can I get dressed, oh Master? Or do you prefer me soaking this growth you laughingly call a floor? Asshole."

Charlie gulped and bobbed his head. He stared at the wall as she disappeared in a puff of smoke and fire. Charlie had barely blinked by the time she returned in another puff of smoke. This time she was dressed in a big, fluffy robe. She reached up and began to rub vigorously at the towel that wrapped her head and hair.

"Alright! That's better. What can I do for you, oh Master?"

She stood one hand on hip and looked disgustedly at Charlie. She shook her head and sighed.

"Shit, a traditionalist. Should'a known. Very well. What are your wishes three, oh Master? But know ye, that there are things your servant mayest not do. The dead shall not be raised. Love may not be granted. And no more than three to a customer. Oh, and I've got limited power so I can only do one wish a week, max. Sorry but it takes me a while to get turned on. So, what was so damn important that I had to cut short my bath for?"

"A ... a ... are you really a Genie?"

"Oh fuck, I got a real winner here. Yes, I'm a real Genie. And no, my name isn't Jeannie and I don't wear harem pants and a halter top. Oh, yeah, and I'm not blue, a cartoon, or speak with the voice of a famous comedian. And you've already seen my belly button and more so enough gawking already. I'm a Jin and the meter's running. Whadda ya want already?"

"Umm, umm, umm," Charlie hummed in confusion.

"Oh shit, let me guess, you didn't realize this was a Genie's bottle. What the frig did you think the burning letters were all about then? Why in the name of all the Powers in the world, did you rub the fracking lamp?"

"It was dirty," squeaked Charlie.

"Shit in this mess, how could you tell?" groused the woman gazing around his apartment.

Story 2 The Sex Jin

"Look, what do I call you? I'm a history student and this bottle looked like an artifact. I was trying to get a closer look. That's all."

"Is that your first wish, to know my name?"

"No, no. I just didn't want to keep calling you Genie."

"Dang," sighed the Genie, "I knew it couldn't be that easy. I've been called a number of things over the ages. Slave – didn't like that one much. Prisoner of the lamp – as if a piece of brass could actually hold me if I wasn't into small house living and it wasn't cheap. Genie – that's usually what I get called. Especially by the less imaginative."

Charlie's cock jumped at the word slave, and he rubbed his thighs together to cover the growing bump in his pants. "No, not what you are but your name," he said.

"Name? What you figure you can bind me for a thousand years, ala Solomon? Really think you got that much power, do you?"

"No,no,no ... a nickname is good enough, just something that I can call you. After all, Genie is what you are not who you are as an individual. And slave ... well, that's just not used in polite company anymore. It's more of a mmm private name between lovers."

The woman gave Charlie a sideways look and then let her eyes trail over him. She stared at his crotch for a moment, and then licked her lips before continuing.

"Tell you what, you can call me Janine. So what's your deep, dark desire, Chuckie boy? What wish can I bring true for you? Money, cars, booze? Sexy women for the night? No love though, strictly one night stands. What's your wish, oh feckless one?"

"Janine, that's a pretty name. Can I call you Jan? I don't know what I want to wish for. How about we start with you sitting down and just talking while I try to decide on my first wish? Would that be okay? That way you don't end up getting tired standing, and I won't get a kink in my neck by staring up at you. Okay, Jan? Please?"

Janine stared at him for a moment and sighed dramatically. With a shake of her head, she headed for the mattress and the only remaining place to sit in the small room. She noticed him staring at her breasts as they swung freely under her robe. She smiled as he licked his lips, and let her eyes caress his handsome face. Not too bad, especially since she'd been cut off for something like fifty years, she thought. At the mattress, she pushed a stack of books with titles like 'Sex Slave Set', 'What Mistress Wants', 'What Her Master Demands' and 'A Taste for the Night' onto the floor. She smiled to herself as she noticed that while a large portion of the books dealt with forced sex or sexual bondage, they were more or less evenly split between male and female as the dominant partner. She smiled and looked Charlie up and down.

Janine sniffed at the dirty mattress formerly hidden beneath the books and grimaced at the thought of sitting there. With a twist of her fingers, the cloth flared. A small pile of dirt appeared beside the pile of books on the floor. Another twist of her fingers and the pile of books flew into a neat stack along the bottom of the bookshelf. Janine brushed fastidiously at the now clean cloth of the mattress cover.

Janine slid into a cross-legged position on the mattress across from Charlie. She knew he could see her thighs beneath the white cloth and while he couldn't quite see into the shadows at the top of her thighs, he would get enough of a flash of skin that it would be obvious she wore nothing under her robe. Janine giggled to herself. A handsome master after 50 odd years of enforced celibacy was just what the physician ordered. Teasing him was going to be fun. She shook her shoulders to adjust the fall of her robe over her cleavage. His gasp as her bare breasts peaked out and then hid again sent a burning sensation flooding from between her legs. Her nipples hardened into tight little buds that burned through the thick cotton of her robe. Janine took a quick glance at his crotch and smiled as she noted the growing bulge. Not a donkey, but more than adequate, she thought to herself.

"Okay, wadda ya want to know, oh Master mine?"

"Look, can you call me Charlie, please? Just Charlie. Not master or anything like that. And I want to know all about you. Where do you come from? How old are you? How did you become a Genie? And how did you get trapped in the lamp? And ..."

Story 2 The Sex Jin

"Hold it. Hold it right there, Charlie boy. First, you never ask a lady her age. Especially ladies who can turn you to a pillar of salt as quick as look at you. Second, if you ask me twenty questions, I might remember one of them. If you want conversation, let's talk. You ask me a question, I answer. Then I ask you a question, and you answer. That's how conversation works. Got it?"

"Umm ... yeah. Sorry. I didn't mean to insult you. I'm just not very good with this. Most girls won't talk to me. It's just I want to know all about you and these questions just keep flowing, you know. Okay, the age question is out. So, where are you from?"

"Good. Nice pickup line there, Casanova. Originally from a small village outside Baghdad. That's in Iran now. Used to be part of the Persian Empire when I was there. Now I kind of bounce around wherever the bottle goes. Travelled quite a bit over the last thousand years or so. Kinda prefer that. Small house living and all that. My turn to ask a question now. See how this works? Okay, what are you doing in a shit-hole like this, Charlie?"

"Well, it's not that bad really. Okay, yes it really is that bad. But it's all I can afford. Nobody wants to hire a history student. Especially one who majored in ancient Middle-Eastern history – Babylon and the early Israelites and so on. And my vacuum broke and I can't afford to fix it and ... well. Ummm ... can I ask now? How did you become a Genie?"

"Well, Daddy and Mommy got together and did the hump-hump and 9 months later, out popped a little Genie. How did you think I'd become a Genie? I was born that way, jerkface. Mom, bless her human soul, didn't notice right away. But by the time I was hitting puberty, enough strangeness was happening that everyone knew what I was. So when Dad popped out of his bottle long enough to visit, I took off and lived with him for an eon or two. Now, my turn with the hard questions. How come your girlfriend allows you to get away with living in a pigsty like this? "

"I'm sorry; I didn't mean to make you uncomfortable. And I don't have a girlfriend. I've never had a girlfriend. Girls just don't like me. I don't have a fancy car. And I can't take them dining and dancing. And I can't buy them fancy jewels and things. So they don't like me. I just don't have enough money for them. "

Story 2 The Sex Jin

"Oooo ... does that mean you're a virgin? I like virgins," Janine purred as she leaned over and spread her hot palm on his thigh. She could feel her breasts swinging free in the robe. Her nipples hardened as they rubbed against the fluffy cotton. She smiled, as she noted that his eyes were glued on the view down her robe.

"Umm ... well, umm ... uh"

Janine swung up onto all fours and crawled along his body. Her hand slid up along his thigh until it rested beside the hard bump in his pants. She could feel his heat and she knew that he, in his turn, could feel the heat from her hand burning into his prick. Her hand flicked and a bright flash painted Charlie's body. A pile of dirt appeared beside the first pile of dirt. Janine smiled a predatory smile.

"So sweet cheeks, let's get this wish thing over with so we can go on to more pleasurable pursuits."

"Well, uhhh ... I still haven't uhh ..."

Charlie shifted in his chair. His prick was so hard it ached. Her hand was like fire on his body. He rubbed his hand along his thigh and groaned.

Janine leaned against him, her breasts fitting around his leg and her thighs spread. One hand rested on his groin, almost but not quite touching the mound of his hard cock. The other clutched at the back of his calf. She licked her lips and lowered her head to rest it on Charlie's thigh. Her hot breath flowed over his crotch. Charlie's hand curled into a tight fist where it rested on his hip. His body was rigid and his breath came in quick, little gulps.

Janine smiled. Her own breath was ragged and she could feel the tight little nobs crowning her breasts pushing into the soft cotton of her robe. Her pussy lips felt slick and the little button at its top was swollen and hard. Her groin clenched and rolled. Janine licked her lips and stared hard at the bump between Charlie's legs.

"Any ideas for what you'd like to wish for, huh? Okay, then let's leave that for a moment and work on my wishes."

Story 2 The Sex Jin

Janine could hear Charlie's gulp as she turned her head and bit down on his thigh through his pants. She ran her hands up his legs as she nibbled her way to the mound tenting his pants. Quickly at first, but with a shudder she reasserted control and then caressed his body more slowly. The rough feel of his jeans against her palms sent jolts of heat flaring up her arms and over her chest. Janine mouthed at the mound, humming to herself as she imagined the taste of his flesh. She ran the tips of her fingernails down his pants and giggled as Charlie cried out. She reached over to her robe and tugged on the ribbon of cotton that secured the white cotton wrap to her waist. A single tug and the cloth parted, revealing her soft, tanned body. A shrug of her shoulders and the robe slipped off to puddle across her calves.

Janine slid her hands up her body until she cupped her breasts. Her fingers flicked the hard brown nobs while she pressed her soft flesh against his leg. When Charlie groaned, she felt her pussy erupt a flow of hot liquid that slid down her leg. Janine whimpered and blinked as waves of desire flooded her body.

Her hands seemed to flow of their own accord, over Charlie's legs and groin until they seized his belt. They fought with the metal for a few moments while

Janine sucked on Charlie's hard cock through his jeans. With the hiss of metal, Janine triumphed and peeled Charlie's pants away from his groin.

Janine's eyes grew bright as Charlie's hard cock pushed its way above the waistband of his briefs. She opened her mouth wide and dove on the pink mushroom of its head. Charlie's head flew back at the feel of her hot, wet mouth surrounding his glans and her lips pressing against his groin. He moaned at each flick of her tongue across the soft sensitive flesh. Janine's fingers scrabbled at the waistband of Charlie's underwear, tearing it down his body. With a hiss of frustration, Janine's fingers twisted and Charlie's clothes disappeared in a puff of smoke.

Janine's tongue flicked out and she ran it along Charlie's pulsing shaft. Charlie's head snapped forward and back, a bobbleheaded metronome bouncing to each wave of sensation from her tongue. Janine glanced up at his face and smiled. She clasped his cock in her teeth and scraped down his rod, her tongue tracing tickling touches behind. She stuck her tongue out and laved over his balls, humming to herself at his cries of pleasure.

Janine hummed at the slight taste of salt and clean skin. Her nose filled with the warm scent of excited man flesh. She twirled her tongue into the folds of his scrotum. With a happy sigh, she sucked one ball into her mouth and sucked on it, her tongue flicking over the hard bulb of salty candy. Charlie's hands clutched at his shaking thigh in response and he groaned. His cock jumped and he gasped as her tongue flicked along his perineum.

Janine slid her hand over Charlie's groin. Her fingers played in the growth of hair for a moment and then slid lower. She grasped his hard cock and squeezed hard. Charlie whimpered and she began to slide her hand up and down the hard shaft. Her fingers squeezed as they bumped over the thick veins. As she felt her palm slide over the soft skin of his glans, she flicked her fingers along the softness. Her palm soon grew damp from the wetness that grew in the slot that topped his hardness. Then quickly downwards smoothing the damp liquid along his rod, squeezing tightly as her hand bounced against her cheek.

Janine gently expelled the hard nut from her mouth. Her teeth grasped the soft skin of his scrotum and pulled back, stretching the skin. One hand continued to pump on his shaft. With a giggle, Janine brought her other hand to between Charlie's legs. Her fingers flicked along the stretched skin of his ball sack. She twisted her head, stretching the skin, first in one direction and then the other. Her fingers continued to tease the stretched skin until Charlie began to cry out in his need.

Janine could feel Charlie's cock leaping in her hand as he approached his climax. But it was too soon. After 50 years, she had no intention of giving up the taste of man this quickly. She opened her mouth and the skin slowly slipped over her lips. She pulled both hands away from him and seized his ass.

Charlie's hips bounced beneath her. His hands seized her head and tried unsuccessfully to push her head back to his crotch. Above her, Janine could hear him sobbing in frustration and pleading with her to continue. She smiled and shifted her hips. She could feel her lips sliding together, the lubricating fluids bubbling over the edge of her lips and flowing down her ass and thighs.

Charlie's chest heaved and it seemed to take forever for his body to stop jerking. The seizures came in waves that lifted his hips and turned his thighs rigid.

Janine tried to control her own needs but no sooner had the spasms stopped than she attacked him once again. A raptor's cry erupted from her mouth as she flew to his hard penis.

Janine swallowed his rod in one deep gulp. She could feel the soft bulb at the end bounce against the back of her throat and she tried not to gag. Her tongue flicked along the shaft and she hummed, pushing the hard rod against the top of her mouth.

Janine seized his balls in one hand. She pulled on them, gently at first, stretching the sack as far as she could. Her hand moved in a semblance of masturbation, stretching the bag of jewels and then releasing it. Stretching him until he was ready to cry out in pain then releasing the pressure. Squeezing the round rocks together between her fingers.

Meanwhile, Janine's head bounced up and down Charlie's shaft. Upwards until the soft mushroom at the top almost escaped her lips. Then downward until the cap mashed against her throat. Her tongue flicked along the shaft throughout the pumping motion. Flicking along the soft, rolled skin of his foreskin. Tracing the purple veins that lined his hardness.

Janine's other hand reached up to tweak at his hard little nipples. She ran her palm over Charlie's stomach and chest, slowly edging her way up until she reached the hard nobs that were her goal. She grasped the hard little bud and squeezed. Her fingers rolled the crinkled flesh as Charlie groaned in response.

Janine nibbled her way down Charlie's shaft. Her sharp little teeth soon turned his skin into a flaming shaft. Her tongue laved over the hard, hotness, cooling the outer fire while building the heat that pumped within the shaft.

Charlie was crying now, and his hips rolled beneath Janine's head. She no longer needed to pull on his sack. Charlie was doing that himself. Stretching his skin until the pressure almost turned to pain. Pulling on her hand as she fought to keep herself in place against his strength.

Janine's own body was twisting now. Her nipples were hard nobs on the ends of her shaking tits. Her boobs shook with every inhalation. Her breath came in uneven, ragged gasps as her chest swelled and fell. Her hips were shaking now, and the liquid need flowed down her legs in a stream. The hard button at the top of her slit was swollen and burned with desire. She could feel her insides clenching and rolling, as they demanded something, anything to fill the void between her legs.

Janine raised her head until her mouth just covered Charlie's glans. She sucked hard on the soft springy flesh, willing the cream to boil up from the balls she was squeezing. Her tongue flicked over and around the head. With a moan, she buried his hard shaft deep in her mouth, the soft tip mashed against her throat. Her cheeks worked as she suctioned on his hardness.

Charlie screamed and his body jerked. His hands pressed on Janine's head, forcing himself deeper into her throat. Janine, in her turn, sucked harder, driving him as far down her throat as she could. White cream erupted from his shaft and sprayed down her gullet. She rode his bucking cock letting the shaft slide slowly out of her mouth. White cream bubbled around her lips and flowed down her chin. She hummed in pleasure at the taste of salt and sugar. Her tongue laved his rod, sucking in the white cream. Janine wiped the overflow with her finger and then sucked on the wetness. She moaned as she sucked on her finger.

Janine gazed up at Charlie. His head lolled and his eyes were crossed. His breathing was ragged and he shivered and gasped. Janine licked her lips, then bent down and gently kissed his still hard prick. She flicked her tongue over the shaft, sucking up the last of the cream, and then kissed her way down to his balls. Her tongue slid over the soft skin of his ball sack. Janine gazed up at Charlie and licked her lips. A mischievous smile spread across her red lips.

"Now, it's my turn – Master."

3. Cyber Sexed

Preface

When I started this series, I conceived of it as a collection of my three non-erotica loves – science fiction, fantasy, and steampunk – combined with erotica. There are several standard themes in each of those three. In science fiction, the space opera and the dystopia future are two of those standard stories. Dystopian SF portrays a future that no sane person actually wants to see happen.

I naturally had to try my hand at both of these standards. With my own twist of course.

Space opera appeared in Book 1 and I now present my view of a dystopian future. I have no idea where this story came from, it just appeared. They do that sometimes. If only so writers can blame the muses when story ideas don't appear.

Hope you enjoy it.

Cyber Sexed

Jennifer stepped delicately over the body twitching on the dirty cement of the platform. She squeezed her way to the back of the crowd waiting for the next train and tried hard not to stare back at the moaning form. A scream ripped her eyes back to the woman who lay, back arched and rigid on the floor. The young woman's nipples were sharp points poking clearly through the translucent silk of her blouse. A large wet spot grew between her legs, staining the pale blue silk skirt that was hiked well above her knees.

Jennifer shivered and looked away. Poor girl, she thought, imagine being caught in public when the chip was turned on. How embarrassing. Everyone would know that her pleasure cycles were out of step. God, that was rough. At least, she wasn't caught in public during a fertility session.

Jennifer closed her eyes to the image flashing across her mind. The image of the woman being held down while all the males in a twenty foot circle were turned into ravenous beasts, ripping off their clothes and attacking her with only a single thought. The image of men sticking their hard cocks in every possible orifice, lining up for a chance to release their hot sticky cum in her soft body. Jennifer shivered and rubbed at the hard plug in the back of her neck. She could feel her pussy clenching at the thoughts ripping through her mind.

The squeal of train brakes ripped through her daydreams. Jennifer forced her feet to march forward the ten feet or so that the exchange of passengers allowed. She stared at the back of the person in front and forced her mind to focus on work, the weather, anything but the scene behind her.

The tube ride was uneventful. Jennifer stood, crammed in the tiny car with several hundred others. Every jolt was emphasized by the squeezing bodies. At least, she hadn't been stuck between perverts this time. The last two rides had been marked by people who held their hands at crotch height. Every bump had pushed hands into her crotch and ass. And the short guy that kept bumping into her breasts was even worse. Jennifer sighed, thoughts of the good old days before muscle toning and genetic treatments were commonplace flickered through her mind. That was when layers of material kept breasts from bouncing or sagging and also provided protection from unwanted contact. At least her breasts were as good as money could buy, so the creeps enjoyed their few seconds of copping a feel. She wondered, not for the first time, what the creeps would think if they knew their few seconds of touch could have landed them in the Pleasure & Pain Rehabilitation Center with just a word from her.

At her stop, she flowed out with the crowd and soon found herself trapped in the elevator. The crush of people had her gasping for air by the time the elevator stopped on the two hundredth floor. Jennifer shivered as she stumbled out into the relatively clear space of the executive offices. She could feel the vein in her neck pulsing and a scream bubbling up inside her throat. In what lately had become a daily ritual, she closed her eyes tightly as she focused on calming nerves burned raw by the press of bodies around her.

Jennifer shook herself deliberately and marched forward into the office, her five-inch stilettos clicking on the tile floor. She strode past the tiny desks lined up in the office. Past the men and women, their heads down, staring at the numbers flashing over the surface of their desks. Past the sign with the flashing numbers that proudly proclaimed "Emergency Pleasure Cycles today" and the other with "Emergency Fertility Cycles this week". Jennifer could feel her perfect breasts quivering and bouncing beneath her transparent top as she marched past her minions. She smiled at the thought of these people taking quick, guilty peeks at her bouncing tits as she flounced past, her black linen skirt flashing glimpses of thigh to anyone bold enough to look.

      Jennifer squeezed herself between the walls that guarded her little cubicle. The sunlight from the full-length window burned her retinas and she twiddled the controls until the light was bearable. Being senior executive in charge of the Department for Sexual Control for this population center had its perquisites. Unfortunately, an office in the corner was a traditional one of them. Which was great, if you liked sunlight and open spaces. Jennifer shuddered and looked away from the dizzying view.

      Jennifer passed her hand over the surface of her desk. It flared for a moment and then settled into a pattern of graphs and messages. Pleasure cycles and variations, fertility cycles and variances, all the key indications of a population center under proper sexual control floated around her desk. Most were green with the occasional flashes of yellow and red. But over in one corner was a graph that flashed bright red. It read "Violence and Service Disruption" in small letters below it.

Story 3 Cyber Sexed

Jennifer tapped her fingers against the graph and her desk flared once again. Now it showed a number of smaller graphs, many pulsating in red, and a display of text. She ignored the manager's explanation that stood at the top of the list. It was bound to be filled with ass covering. Instead, she quickly scanned down the list of occurrences looking for an explanation of the high ratings in violence.

It took Jennifer a scant few minutes to identify the pattern. The Sexual Freedomists, the so-called SexFrees, were disrupting pleasure cycles and replacing them with fertility cycles. The attacks weren't enough to affect the predicted population numbers yet but if they ignored the problem, the effect on population would be felt. Jennifer shuddered. The idea of even more people trying to access the limited resources of the population center was frightening. Something needed to be done about these fanatics and now.

Jennifer sat at her desk, rippling her fingernails across the glass. She knew the tattoo irritated the others near her office but she didn't care. Right now her irritation was quite frankly more important. That was one of the nice benefits of being the boss. She sniffed and straightened her chair.

Two touches at her desk brought up the image of the Senior Director for Stability.

"Georgina, it's Jenn. We have a major problem and I need you to solve it. Quickly. These damn SexFrees have been disrupting our cycles. Planning is difficult under the best of times. But under these circumstances, frankly, I don't know how my people are keeping the population stable. I don't care what you do but you need to remove them from the board. Permanently."

"Yes, Madam Senior Executive. We've been trying, but I'm afraid it hasn't been as easy as it should be. They seem to have inside help. We've been picking up rumors of a major initiative but haven't been able to pin down exactly what they are planning. For some reason their stability observation circuits aren't working. We aren't hearing them when they plan their attacks."

"I don't care about your excuses. Just smash these upstarts. Sexual freedom indeed. And where has sexual freedom gotten us, I ask you? Squeezed into tiny spaces and over use of what little resources we have left. The invention of the SR chip was the best thing that ever happened to the human race. I want them smashed so we can go back to our controlled lives. Do you hear me? You have two day cycles."

Jennifer slammed her palm down on the picture, banishing it to the net and leaving her palm tingling and burning. She leaned back in her chair and rubbed her hand across the plug in the back of her neck that was the maintenance port for her own chip. She wondered for the fiftieth time that morning if her chip was malfunctioning and burning up her neck. She decided that she would go see the tech team one floor down. They'd jump to check out her port and chip. After all, keeping the boss happy was job number one. And there were plenty others where they came from.

That was only right. After all, a malfunctioning port would leave her vulnerable with no way to maintain her chip. She could feel her own nipples hardening at the thought of uncontrolled sexuality. Imagine being caught like that poor woman this morning in a cycle of unconstrained demand with no way to turn the chip off. With a shiver, she put the thought out of her mind and forced her thoughts back to the work sitting in her overflowing inbox.

As Jennifer worked through the many requests, she could feel her legs moving seemingly of their own accord. They shifted up and down, forcing her thighs to rub over her groin. She twisted and wreathed as she felt a prickling heat flood over her chest. Jennifer reached up to rub at the burning in her neck and jerked her fingers back from the fiery metal insert. She blew on her fingers and then reached into her purse to pull out a small round compact. A small bit of contortion was all that was needed to see the back of her neck reflected in the mirror and bounced off the reflective surface of her desk. The metal connection was blackened and a small trail of smoke rose from the hole in the center.

Jennifer threw her compact on the desk in disgust. She knew she should have gone down to maintenance earlier, but with her workload, she didn't really have the time. Jennifer groaned in frustration. She smoothed her transparent blouse over her ample chest and then ran her hand over her black linen skirt. She whimpered as her hands flicked over her hard nipples. They burned and tightened further. Traces of fire radiated outward over her tits. Her hand slipping down the fleshy thigh bordering her pussy drew a gasp from her lungs. Jennifer blinked in confusion.

Story 3 Cyber Sexed

Jennifer shuddered and stared from under her brows as the massive figure of Jerome from Perversion Suppression filled her office door. Her eyes flicked over his rugged face and wide, muscular chest, finally coming to rest staring at his crotch. She licked her lips at the sight of the mounded white wool cloth right at her eye height.

"Madam Senior Executive, I'd like to speak with you for a moment. My team has noticed a sharp uptick in unsanctioned, non-BDSM sexual unions. Every one of my teams is breaking up at least six orgies a day now. It's just too much. We're not just hands-off Doms and Subs in this department, you know. We often have to get right in there. We're selected for the greatest sexual endurance and organ reactivity. But it's just too much. We're only human. I need at least five more teams if this continues just to keep up. Plus, I'm going to have to start cycling teams into recovery soon and when that happens, I'll need at least five more on top of that. I need a special executive order to hire more Suppressors. And I need it now."

Jennifer smiled seductively up at Jerome. She licked her lips and then shook her head to clear the fog. Suppression teams, he said something about more suppression teams. What could he be wanting to suppress, she wondered. His desires? Her desires? Jennifer blinked slowly, trying to concentrate. Dom or Sub? Dom could be an interesting battle for power. But Sub would be fun too. The burning sensation had spread outward from her nipples and her whole face now burned. She could feel liquid bubbling out from between her tightly clasped legs, and she gasped as a ripple of desire rolled over her lower body.

"Madame Senior Executive, is there something wrong? I need those Suppression teams and I need to start training them immediately. But first, I need you to authorize the extra teams. Madame Senior Executive? Umm ..."

Jennifer followed his shifting hips with eyes that seemed glued to the slowly enlarging mound that swelled one of his thighs. She sighed and licked her lips. Her hands shifted uncontrollably on her thighs, clutching at the soft material and pulling her hemline higher. Her own hips were rolling and twisting in her chair and she could feel her lips slipping over each other and pulling on the now hard bud between them. The feel of the silk rubbing over her hard nipples was sending rolling waves of fire over her tits. Jennifer shook her head, and moaned.

Jennifer's hands seemed to move of their own accord, reaching out and seizing Jerome's hips, pulling him in closer. Her eyes noted that his hands slid behind his slowly heaving hips to rest on his round ass cheeks. She grinned. A Sub, definitely a Sub, she thought in flashes of desire. Her hands caressed his groin through his pants finally coming to rest on the black belt that held his white wool pants. Her hands shook as she fought with the clasp. She moaned as the belt fell away and her hands reached for the zipper. The mound that ran down his thigh was pushing against the cloth now. It was obvious in its hardness, long and thick. Jennifer licked her lips as she flashed on a memory of the taste of hard man flesh. Of the feel of softness and salt against her tongue. Of the wetness of the tip sliding over her tongue. She moaned loudly.

Jennifer's hands were shaking as she peeled the cloth back from his bare groin. The soft skin was bare. She could clearly see the rippled skin where his manhood was bent and forced down the leg of his pants. She groaned as she licked across his groin, loving the feeling of bare skin and the tiny prickles where his shaving wasn't quite close enough. She hummed at the light taste of salt from his skin. Her tongue flicked out, quickly lapping at the mound of skin at the base of his prick. Jerome groaned and shook as the hot, wet feel of her tongue teased at his hardness. His cock jerked, tenting his pant leg even further.

Jennifer grinned up at Jerome's grimacing face. She opened her mouth wide and bit down on his hard shaft where it bent to enter his body on the one end and his pant leg on the other. Jerome groaned loudly and pushed his hips toward her. She bounced for a moment, her teeth caressing him. She pulled on his pants forcing them down until just the pink tip of his cock was covered. She sucked and pulled on his cock until it sprung free and his pants tumbled down to pool at his feet.

Jennifer could feel his hard prick bouncing against her cheek in its eagerness to escape the confinement. She ran her tongue along his hard shaft until she reached the soft tip. She moaned as her head bobbed and she swallowed his hardness until it bounced against the back of her throat. She hummed and slowly drew her lips up the rod. Her teeth lightly bounced off the hardness. The salty sweet taste of his manhood filled her mouth as she sucked hard on his soft skin.

Her tongue slid around the bulb, tickling the soft folds of skin. She pushed her tongue into the depression she found at the top of his prick, tasting the salty sweet of his pre-cum. She pushed the tip of her tongue deeply into the hole, fucking him with her tongue in a turnabout that she knew would not be lost on him. Her head bobbed once again until his bulb was crushed against her throat.

She sucked on his hardness and ran her tongue around the hard shaft until she began to see stars. With a gasp of life-giving air she tore her mouth off his prick. Her head bobbed once again but this time she pushed her jaw against his balls. She sucked the soft flesh into her mouth. Her tongue flicked over the soft folds, twisting the skin into little circles.

Her tongue slid over the soft skin of his groin, circling his jerking cock. Jerome groaned and then cried out. His cock jerked hard, spitting a long stream of white cum along her cheek and into her hair. It jerked again and again, smashing against her cheek and spraying cream deep into her hair. Jennifer growled.

"Did I give you leave to come? Did I, scum? You need some of your own vaunted training. Shall I train you, prick? Shall I?"

"Oh fuck yes, Mistress. Please train me. Please make me your pleasure slave."

"Down on your knees. It's time to pleasure me. Your mouth only. I want to feel your mouth stripping my panties down. Think you can handle that, scum?"

"Yes, Mistress."

"Then do it and do it good or I'll take a whip to that shriveled little sausage you laughingly call a prick."

Jennifer sighed as she watched Jerome drop to his knees at her feet. She leaned back and closed her eyes. She could feel his coarse cheeks rub along her soft thighs. She felt his chin rub against her clit through the silk panties as he plucked at her underclothes with his teeth. Jennifer grabbed the back of his head and forced his face further into her body. She shivered as she felt the material pulling down over her soft naked flesh.

Jennifer lifted her hips as she felt the cloth slide down. Teasing was fine but she could feel her lips overflowing, the juices running down her ass to puddle on the chair. She could feel her tiny bud burning with need. Jerome fought with the cloth for a moment, stretching her panties over her ample ass and then pulling the silk down her thighs and calves. He licked his way from her ankles to her crotch as Jennifer moaned. Her hips bucked as she felt his tongue slip between her lips. She gasped and gave herself up to the feel of his tongue on her most sensitive parts.

Jennifer groaned as she felt a mouth clamp onto her nipple through the silk of her blouse. Moments later cold hit her other breast as her blouse was ripped open. A tongue flicked over the hard red bud that crowned her soft white tit. It was quickly followed by the hot moistness of a suckling mouth. She moaned and shivered. It took a moment for the sensations and contradictions to trickle through to her brain. When it did her eyes flared open and she stared around her.

John from Sexual Statistics knelt to one side, suckling her breast through the silk blouse. His bald head bobbed in rhythm to his sucking and the flicking of his tongue against her hard nipple. His hands softly kneaded at her flesh, elongating the tit and drawing the flesh into his mouth. His shirt was torn open and his pants were in an untidy pile beneath his knees. His cock was hard and stood straight out from the black bush at his crotch.

Susanne from Fantasy Investigations was chewing on her other breast. Her blouse was ripped open and her firm tits swung freely with every movement. One hand slowly massaged Jennifer's tummy. The other hand was buried beneath Suzanne's rolled up skirt. It pumped slowly as Suzanne pushed against the flesh between her legs. Her sharp teeth skimmed the soft skin of Jennifer's tit, burning the whiteness. She nibbled along the edges of Jennifer's hard nipple sending flashes of fire flowing over Jennifer's breast. Jennifer shivered beneath the onslaught.

Sam from R&D was pulling his shirt over his head while he tripped over the pile of his pants that had slipped down to his ankles. His chest was ripped and a six pack was clearly visible on his stomach. The muscles stretched into a V that nicely framed the hard cock that bounced from his naked groin. As his shirt flew off his head, he reached out and ran his hand along Jerome's naked ass. His hands gripped the cheek leaving white hemisphere's burned into the flesh.

Jennifer sensed rather than saw a fifth body beneath Jerome. She couldn't tell who it was but his cock was hard and thick and stood straight up. It slid along Jerome's thigh leaving a trail of wetness. His hand had found John's cock and was absent-mindedly stripping up and down. The feel of a tongue sliding on her ass while Jerome's tongue continued to flick at her clit and inner lips was almost more than she could stand.

Jennifer flung her head back and screamed as the first of several climaxes tore through her body. Her thighs clenched. Her ass slid forward on the chair and the tongue slid further into the channel between her cheeks. It twirled around the crinkled skin at first and then pushed within the tight sphincter to lick and push in a mad parody of fucking. Jerome's tongue slipped up her cunt from the entrance to her clit. He sucked on her lips, drawing the flesh deep into his mouth while his tongue teased at her flesh. She could feel his teeth sliding on the sensitive flesh sending flares of sensation rippling outwards. Jennifer's head bounced back and forwards as the roll waves of her clenching flesh tumbled over her. A river of cum flooded out of her pussy and dripped on the chest of the unknown man beneath her.

Jennifer's eyes slowly cracked open as the waves of pleasure receded into building waves of mere sensation and desire. Her brain slid between focus and awareness. She stared at the entrance to her small office. At least twenty people were crammed into the small space that guarded her doorway. She could see flashes of flesh – breasts and cocks, thighs and arms, chests and pussies. A writhing mass of flesh fighting to reach her. Fighting to pleasure her. Fighting to fuck her. Her eyes flicked to take in the colors of bushes and the hard softness of bare groins. Her mouth opened and she panted as she felt her need spike.

Waves of sensation flooded over her as her mind shut down to anything except the climax and the burning in her nipples and clit. She could feel her pussy grinding as it sought a cock that wasn't there. A cock she knew would soon fill her. All she had to do was choose between the frantic offerings around her.

Jennifer smiled. This was going to be fun. Fuck the repair depot. Who needed an off switch anyway?

4. Swords and Sexery

Preface

I've already introduced you to Hassan and his rather dangerous wife, and the three stories they have generated so far (see my intro to The Sex Jin). By the way, the reason I keep referring to Hassan's wife as Hassan's wife rather than by her name is that he was so important a character that I didn't even bother to name his family (or even fill out the numbers). In fact, I barely decided that his wife was a swordsmistress and that he had more than one daughter. So much as it offends me, all I have is Hassan and a fuzzy wife off somewhere.

So this story started life as an attempt to give Hassan's wife a life of her own. It didn't quite work that way. At least it hasn't at the moment – maybe she'll do the playing around when I get to his story. We shall see.

I actually came up with the title to this piece first before the story and the influence of Hassan's wife. In fantasy there is a branch called Swords and Sorcery. It's populated by big hairy men (and a few big hairy women) with big swords and very few brains. It's also populated by rather slimy wizards and sorcerers. Thus the name S & S fantasy. The bar fight and tavern scene are two staples in this sub-genre. After all, barbarians have to be heavy drinkers, don't they?

Since I write erotica, I tweaked that to be Swords and Sex (which later morphed to Sexery in order to rhyme with Sorcery). And I wanted to write a tavern scene. Of course, my hero had to be a woman. A horny woman. Have to keep honest to my roots after all. Along comes Hassan's wife, and Shara and the story was born.

I hate first person stories. I don't like to read them and I don't like to write them. They sound pretentious to me. As if the writer is trying to pretend they are a friend telling a tale. As writers, we need to tell a tale differently from a gossip tale with a friend. We need to include description, we need to include story elements, we need to include interesting characters. None of which is needed when a bunch of friends are sitting around gossiping. And all of which tend to push a first person story over the edge of pretention into that squirmy, smarmy give-me-a-break level of writing.

Of course, this story decided that my preferences were irrelevant.

Story 4 Swords and Sexery

Interestingly, this story was written in a single sit-down within a two hour period from glimmer of an idea to finished manuscript. That's about half the time I usually take to just write a fully formed story. It was determined to get out and be written in its own fashion. And it did.

After which, I had a killer craving for a beer. And a session with my husband, Toy.

Swords and Sexery

It wasn't much of a tavern. Just a spot between two old walls with a tarp thrown over it and a couple of benches. Oh yeah, there were a couple of tables and a few boxes that served as the bar. That's all. Nothing special. On rainy days, the crud from the streets flowed down the alley and formed a river underneath the feet of the guests. But at least the tarp kept most of the rain out of the beer. And it was good beer. Honest ha'penny beer. It wasn't much of a tavern but the beer was good and cheap. And there was always lots of it. But mostly it was my tavern.

Oh, I don't mean I owned it; if anyone could be said to own a squalid squat like that. I mean it was where I spent my time. Hell, I even had my own bench. With a table, even. And the wenches knew me. They'd pass me an extra brew on the side to keep the worst of the drunks worrying about their necks and not their pricks if you know what I mean. A good place. My place.

She shouldn't ought to have wrecked it like that.

I guess, I should start at the beginning. Name's Shara. I'm what you might call a warrior woman. Mostly I just heave a bloody big ax around while wearing just enough chain mail to keep the priests off my back. After all, no one wants their decency patrols on her back. At least not in a "you're under arrest" kind of way. But I also want to keep the covering down to little enough chain mail that it'll distract my male opponents. And more than a few of the females. Don't really need the armor. Most males drop their jaws and lift their swords when they see me. Fools never even take a swing. At least not with their metal weapons, if you know what I mean. Hey, I'm not exactly your delicate flower but I got tits and hips that are all in the right places. Real suckable if you catch my drift. Most guys get an instant hardon when they see me and my blonde locks. Especially with all the leather straps it takes to keep my swords and knives in place. Taken my share of admirers, I tell you.

Let me take a swig of this ale. Not bad. Not as good as my place but good ale nonetheless. Now where was I? Oh, yeah. My old place and the bitch. Anyway, I kind of kept the denizens in line with the girls. After all, it's okay if one of the wenches decides she likes a guy and wants to do the bump-bump thing with him. It's her body, you know what I mean. Done it a few times myself. But it isn't cool for a scumbag to force his

Story 4 Swords and Sexery

attentions and some of them cocksuckers needed a little discouragement.

Anyway, that's what happened with this filly. I was sitting in my usual spot, being entertained by one of the cuter swords. We'd just moved to fingers on fun spots and here she comes into the tavern looking all delicate and pretty and stuff. Her with her tiny frame that I could break with one hand and her big tits that an average man couldn't lift even with two hands. And wearing some silky little robe over her dancer's top and bust-catchers. Came in, sat down, and ordered a beer like she was in some kind of snotty upper class place. For a witch, she sure was seven kinds of stupid.

Took about as long as I took to empty this here jug for the sharks to circle. That mug sure is empty. Be real nice if it was full of beer. Real nice of you. Don't mind if I do. As I was saying, she had a half-dozen men circling her in the time it takes to empty a beer. Real cocksmen they were too. At least in their own minds. Not a bath or piece of clean clothing amongst them in a week or more.

Started slavering over her they did. No, I mean literally. They were sucking and licking all over her. They started pawing at her first of course. Their rough hands kept getting caught in her robe. She didn't seem to mind at first so I didn't think too much about it. Rather liked the attention in fact so I reckoned it were none of my business.

One of them began by massaging her neck. You know how men get. They start rubbing our shoulders and cooing about how stiff we are. As if we don't know that it's really about how stiff they're getting. Well, she was really getting into the act. You could actually hear her purr she was enjoying it that much. She was rubbing up against him like some kind of big cat. His hands were slipping up and down her neck and shoulders. He dug his thumbs into her neck muscles and pulled so hard her skin was pushed up into a hill. I'm surprised she wasn't yelping and turning around to hurt him back. And every time he ran those hands over her shoulder, the robe would catch and slip a little lower. Instead of punching him where it would hurt, all she did was let her head droop back and moan. Banging her black ponytail against his fat stomach, she was.

Then another started rubbing at one arm while a third got the other arm. They started out all innocent like at the wrist. Her hands were flopping around like the harbor catch down at Fisherman's Dock. Then they

Story 4 Swords and Sexery

started on her forearms. Her hands were just flying then. Blood rag dolly, let me tell you. All the time, her robe's getting pulled this way and that by their rough hands. Then they moved up to her forearms. Her hands were slapping at their privacies, which was kind of the whole point. At least they thought so, I guess. They were showing what they had and in a couple cases, it was a lot more than I would have given them credit for. Anyway, by the time they had reached her shoulders the silk robe was catching on their rough skin good. The robe was gaping wide open around those red bust-catchers. That strip of red cloth around her tits didn't hide much and you could tell her nips were hard as rocks and pointing to heaven.

That was about when the fourth and fifth guys dropped to their knees in front of her. By this time, the guys at the top had ripped the silk robe into thin strips so these guys didn't have much between them and their goals. Their hands went straight to her upper thigh and they began massaging her leg. They started at the top and worked their way down. Twins they were. Little round squeezes except at the ass where they grabbed great hunks and squeezed. Treating her ass like it was a pair of tits. Pulling her cheeks so far apart it must have felt like her asshole was going to tear apart. Then down the thigh, rubbing and squeezing down to the calf. When they started sucking on her toes I was kind of wondering what was up, you know what I mean? And no, I don't mean their pricks. That was pretty obvious even from my table.

When the sixth guy plopped down in front of her, I just about creamed my breechclout. I mean, shit, there's a time and a place for everything. This area was for beer. There were some boxes piled in back with a straw mattress if you were in a hurry. And a couple of places around here to rent a room if you wanted to take some time to explore your options. It was enough to make a girl gag on her beer. Mind you, the guy I was with didn't seem to mind it when number six started to roll her panties down with his teeth. My guy's fingers were playing a pretty tune under my chain loincloth at the time. And the chain links really began to jangle, let me tell you.

Anyway, by this time, number six has her pants down to her knees and he's kissing his way up her thighs and heading for a drink at the fountain. Number four and five are licking their way up the outside of her calves. And the other three have thrown her clothes on the ground. Two and three are licking and kissing her pretty titties and sucking on those hard brown nobs as if they held honey mead. The guy in back had her bent back and was swabbing her tonsils with his tongue.

Story 4 Swords and Sexery

She's groaning out loud now. Real screamer this one. Her breathing is coming in great gasps and her tits are bouncing, her chest is pumping so hard. She starts scrabbling at two and three's codpieces. She soon had their members out in the cold air. Rather than let them cool down, she starts rubbing them up and down. Every time she hits the balls, she gives them a squeeze and every time she hits the head, it's a flick with her thumb. She's soon got their hips bouncing. They're fucking the air like it was a twenty-guinea whore. Not that he'd have a chance with a twenty-guinea whore, you understand.

The guy behind her has had enough by now. So he pulls his cock out and shoves it down her throat. She's humming in pleasure now. Her tongue is flicking up and down the skin. She's treating it like a candy stick and she's a starving child, she is. I kept waiting for her to bite off a hunk and swallow it whole. All this time her hands are flying on the other guys pricks. I'd swear she's trying to jerk their junk off and throw it away, she's pulling so hard. But they're loving it. They're moaning and shivering.

The guy between her legs is licking his way to heaven. His tongue is dipping in the trough and then traveling up the river until it finds the tree. Then he's sucking on that bud as if it was his mother's teat. And every time he sucks, she bucks and screams.

Now, at this point, I don't mind all that much. Hey, she's hot. What she's doing is hot. And I'm all for hot. Especially when it gets my male harder and gets my juices flowing faster. I like the bump-bump as much as the next girl, after all. It gets in the way of proper drinking but a little bit of entertainment is okay as long as the beer keeps coming.

Problem is that the guys are being entertained a little too much. Every guy in the place is getting up to take a better look. Some of them are getting in the way of my view. Not for long, of course. I suggested that they move and they did. The pile of bodies from those that didn't helped discourage others from getting in my way. Didn't take more than a dozen or so before the others got the hint.

Now some of the other ladies in the tavern were getting upset, but I'm the live and let live type. So I was cool with it. Until I noticed the fingers tickling my pussy weren't moving anymore. When my date got up and started wandering over for a closer look, it was just too much. Hey, a girl's got her reputation to look after. It wasn't right.

So I push the table back and get up. Yeah, now that you mention it, I do remember a couple of guys across from me screaming and grabbing their legs. I figure that they got a little too excited and dropped their load a little early. It happens. Just need to take their equipment out a little more often, that's all.

Anyway, I push my way to the front of the crowd. Couple of the guys try to argue but I convince them quick and easy. You know the old joke. Here's quick. And here's easy. Like that. Anyway I step over the bodies and I've got a clear view to this bimbo.

She's down to nothing, just an iron slave collar around her throat. Her silk dancing outfit is being ground into the dust beneath several dozen feet. She's going to have a real problem getting back home past the priests, that's for sure. Now, I'm not a ladies girl. I like the men too much and I'd rather play with a guy's dangly bits any day. But even I have to admit this is one good looking woman. She's got tits that look like they're about to fly off, a tiny wasp waist, and a bare pussy that was good enough to eat. Just ask the guy who was slobbering over it.

So she sees me gawking at her, my face getting red and the anger just burning behind my eyes. And what does she do? She flips me off. Then she pulls the guy's cock out of her mouth and dares me to a screwing match. Me! Can you imagine the gall of her?

I mean, what can I do? I grab two of the gawkers by the neck and throw them over to the nearest table. I use my bra to tie two more together and my breechclout to tie two more guys and drag them over to the table. Some gawker in a noble's clothes makes for seven. Him I toss on the table. He tries to give me grief so I belt him a good one and lay him out face up. I figure if he does a good job, I might turn him around and let him plow my back forty. But I'm mad at him so he's stuck with a taste.

I jump up on the table and shove my ass in his face. While he can still hear, I explain what I'm expecting. Then it's my ass on his face and he isn't hearing anything for a while. It takes a minute but he gets the idea and I can feel his tongue flicking along the channel. He's licking away at the edges of the entrance and my hips are starting to grind.

I grab the two guys with my bra. I figure they've had a chance to figure out what goes in there so I stick one on each tit. One gets started right away. He's licking around the whole breast. His tongue is like a soft wet cloth and he's giving me a tit bath. The other one just grabs on to the nipple and starts sucking for all he's worth. His mouth is pulling away at my flesh and it's getting harder and harder. It's so hard it's hurting. But it's a good hurt; you know the kind that burns all the way down to my clit. So I push his face further into my tit and just lay back and enjoy his hot wet mouth.

After a few moments, I get bored with this so I grab the guys that borrowed my breechclout. One of them gets laid out with his head between my legs. He gets to licking away. Between his tongue flicking along my pussy and between my legs and the guy in back, I worried for a moment that the guy in back might drown. But then I say fuck it and if a little woman juice is going to be too much for him then he deserves to drown in it. It's still too early for the other guy so I stick him on my clit. His tongue is flicking along the boat and he's pulling the little man out with his mouth. When he starts nibbling on it I just about scream. By this point, my juices are just pouring out and dribbling down over the guy between my legs and the guy in back. Guy in back is choking on it but I grind my ass down anyway and he shoves his tongue into me. The first of my buzz crackers goes off and I'm groaning and rolling my hips.

After a bit, my pussy stops trying to crawl up my spine and I go back to a slow buildup. The folks down below are still at it with their tongues but my hands and mouth are getting a little lonely. The two guys I tossed over first are beginning to wake up so I pull them over. Their pants get a little torn in the process and their codpieces end up around the throat of one of the wenches watching the show. Don't know why she yelled so loud, it wasn't like she'd never had that happen before.

I start pulling on their junk and they're really enjoying it. They're not badly built and I'm stretching them out as far as they'll go. My hand is squeezing all the way and the head is going purple and looking as if it'll burst the next time I pump. Every time my hand buries itself in their cock hair, their balls come swinging out and bounce off my fist. They squeal like a suckling pig looking for its momma. But, it's like squeezing an iron bar so I know they're just appreciating my abilities with my hands.

Story 4 Swords and Sexery

Problem is that my mouth is still empty and I'm out of the guys I seduced when we started this party. So I grab a likely looking candidate from the crowd. Typical nobility, he's just standing there looking arrogant playing with this little key on a chain. But he's kind of cute, you know. Black hair, pointy chin, real elfin face. No beard or mustache, which was unusual in this kind of crowd. In fact, I could have sworn he had just shaved, he had so little evening shadow. Good shoulders, no ax swinger but I could tell he'd swung a few clubs in his time. Tight buns and strong thighs. His cock was hard and had pushed its way out of his codpiece. I could tell he had no need to brag unlike most of the pricks that usually hung around here. Well dressed. In fact, he was a little too well dressed for this part of town. Obviously a rich noble out for a taste of the poor folk. Well this poor folk was going to get a taste of him.

So I let go of one of the guys I'm jerking on, and he's so disappointed he just sort of collapses on my tit. Almost dislodged the guy who I had stuck with the job of sucking my nip. I didn't like that much but the guy on my tit just sucks harder so I figure it's okay for the time it was going to take to grab a taste of the pretty boy.

I grab the noble and rip his codpiece off. It wouldn't come at first but I pulled and the poor sod screams as the straps get caught in his ass. I end up with the cloth ripping and it's just hanging there. One of the nicest pleasure poles I've seen in a while. It's about ten inches long, and a good 6 inches around. Big purple plum on the end and these purple veins puffed out along its length. Too big for the lower mouth on most of these wenches but just right to nibble on for me. And his balls are massive. I grab him and aim him straight for my tonsils. Almost breaks my jaw, but I've got a good chunk in and I'm sucking hard enough the skins rubbing over my tongue.

My hand's getting cold but before I put it back where it belongs, I grab the guy with his tongue on my clit. I pull him up by the hair until he's in the right position and then growl at him on account of my mouths full. He gets the idea and I feel his cock sliding around in the hot and wet. He finally finds the right hole and shoves. His hardness slides right in and I feel it slide past each and every ridge. He may not be as big as the guy in my mouth but he's a good size and he fills me up nicely. He starts pounding and I feel every movement.

The guy in my ass is digging his tongue in nicely. And the guy between my legs is flicking his

Story 4 Swords and Sexery

tongue across my lips. I can feel his tongue flicking between me and the guy who's shafting me. I decide that it doesn't matter to me if he wants to lick a little cock, as long as he continues licking my juices.

So I'm all filled up and all these cocks and tongues are pounding parts of me. I debated if I wanted to grab another couple of bystanders and put them to work on my feet and calves, but I decide that's just being greedy. So I put it off. Hell, if I need to I can always let go and grab a couple volunteers later. Instead, I grab that guy who's sleeping on my tit. His cock has to be getting cold by now and I figure I'll warm it up for him. A little friction soon turns his cold hose into a hot iron rod.

I shift a little bit and settle in for a little fun. The tongue in my ass and the tongue between my legs are both twirling my insides. The cock in my cunt is pounding the sensations up my spine and the mouths on my nips are sucking it out of my tits. The sensations are twirling around between the sisters just like I like it. My hands are having fun pulling on the two sausages in my hands and I'm sucking for all I'm worth on the monster in my mouth. All's right with the world except for one little thing.

The guy I'm sucking on is groaning and shivering. He's grabbed my head, which I'm not a big fan of. But that's okay; I can understand that every time I stick my tongue into the little hole in the tip of his cock, he shivers. And every time I run my tongue over the shaft he groans. But his damn key on a chain keeps hitting me in the nose. And I'm getting tired of it.

So to take my mind off this damn piece of iron, I look over at the dancer chick. Her back is arched like a temple entrance. The guy who was licking her cunt is still there, but he's been joined by another one who is pounding her pussy like he's digging for gold. The guy that had his cock in her mouth has lost it. He's standing there shaking. His cock is jumping like a ringer on the temple bell on a high holiday. The white cum is flying out. Most of it is landing in her mouth and flowing over the sides, but long white streams of it are bouncing off her nipples and stretching over her chin and cheeks to settle in long streaks into her hair. The guys she's pulling on choose that moment to lose their cream. It goes flying over her body and splats against the other guy. Strings of it are dripping off her tits and stomach. She starts screaming and the cum sprays out of her mouth all down her chest while the guy who's pounding her turns on the speed. He's pounding her so hard and fast he's turning into a blur.

Story 4 Swords and Sexery

It's at that moment that the guys I'm yanking on start losing it. Their cream is flying over my chest and landing on the two guys who are licking my tits. The guy in my mouth groans and my mouth fills with white stuff. It's salty, sweet and I've got to swallow it before I drown. Between him and the guy pounding into my own pussy, I hit another climax and my own screams are ripping out over the crowd.

Which is fine, but that damn key chooses that exact moment to smash into my nose. I've had it with that thing, so I grab it in my mouth and bite down. Hard. Didn't think about it, I just ripped into the chain and tore it off. Didn't swallow it just by luck. Spit it out again fortunately.

A moment later and there's this big bolt of lightning come flying over my head. Almost trimmed my eyebrows. I'm still pulling melted hair out of my bangs. Bolt strikes the pretty boy right in the chest. He screams and turns into a cinder. I look over to the dancer and she's up on her knees, the slave collar is hanging off her throat now. She's looking at where the pretty boy was and it isn't a good look. There's enough hatred in that look to butcher, fry and serve your typical bull let alone a dumb noble like pretty boy.

That's when the priests and the decency guards arrived and closed my poor tavern.

5. Well Met in the Forest

Preface

As I mentioned in the book introduction, most of my novels have begun life as a short story. Usually, intentionally.

This is an exception, sort of.

This story started life as a short story. I had a chance to write short stories and get paid for it. The only question was if the pay was worth the amount of time. To see if it was, I wrote two of the three requested stories. Unfortunately, the time involved for the pay offered wasn't worthwhile. A problem most writers can empathize with. So the story languished for several years.

If you read my Steamy Shorts 1 you've seen this intro before. A Taste for the Night began this way. Well, so did Chasing Fae Romance. And from the same experiment. And just like A Taste for the Night this story went on to become a novel and then a series of novels.

In most cases, my titles come first and then the short story. And the story continues to morph through various levels of outline. While the title is supposed to be a working title, it seldom changes by any great amount.

But in this case, the story came first in its final form and then the title came. And came again. And came again. And it wouldn't stop changing until I finally got tired and froze the result out of sheer frustration. At which point it tried to morph once more. I refused. Time will tell if that was the right or wrong decision.

Here you see the story with the original title of Well Met in the Forest. Which led to the series Chasing Fae Romance. And the novel Well Met in Forest Light. And the series titles Well Met in something Light. And you get the idea and a taste of why I was getting frustrated. Meanwhile the story, at the chapter/short story level, book level, and series level stayed the same. It wasn't until I finished the latest novel (Well Met in Castle Light) that the series changed. Maybe – and only because I don't think I can fit the rest of the story in a single book. Of course I could be wrong. In which case the story is still the original. Which will fry my poor writer's brain.

Story 5 Chasing Fae Romance

So here's the original story that launched Well Met in Forest Light Book 1 of the Chasing Fae Romance series available in Kindle format from Amazon with its original title. I hope you enjoy it.

Well Met in the Forest

There is a hypnotic quality to the rhythmic slap of rubber sole on hard packed earth and a melody buried in the woosh of a runner's breathing. Sarah allowed the music of her running to soothe her mind. A run through the wooded parkland was a critical part of Sarah's morning routine. The slight hills of the path gave her enough exercise to leave her energized but not so tired that she wanted to go back to bed. And the privacy and beauty of the woods and streams helped to clear her mind and remove the fears that might infect her day. As a rising young entrepreneur, she needed to be eager and confident. Fear was a luxury that she simply couldn't afford.

Sarah took a deep breath through her nose, inhaling the scent of the autumn fog, the smell of moisture, mold, trees, and soil that was unique to this time of day. In a few short hours, the sun would burn off the fog, and the sickly aroma of the city's love of the car would infect her oasis of calm. But for the moment, she could imagine that the parkland was ancient forest and that the city was far away.

Sarah focused on her run and began to speed up as she ran down the slight grade leading to the stream and the cute little bridge that marked the halfway point of her run. She let her mind be seized by the slight bouncing of her firm, bountiful breasts in the bra of the crop top she wore. Gravity grabbed and pulled at her tits, lightly caressing the nipples against the Lycra. The slap of her blonde ponytail against her back tapped a counterpoint to the bouncing of her tits. The feel of the sweat running down her belly and between the lips of her pussy cemented the direction her mind ran.

"Six months is too long," she thought as she felt her skin slide in the moisture. "If I don't find a man soon, I'm going to go nuts. I'm getting real tired of being married to a piece of plastic."

The meadow around the stream was dappled in the pre-dawn light with tendrils of fog oozing between the trees almost obscuring the bridge and the large stone with the plaque. Sarah almost screamed as she burst from the trees and spotted the figure resting on the stone.

Story 5 Chasing Fae Romance

"Ah, fuck. It's hard enough to meditate when I'm horny. What do I get? Some perv looking to give me a hard time. Well, bring it on. If I can't get a man in my own bed then I'm going to put one in a hospital bed. Either way will cool me down and get my mind out of the gutter," Sarah whispered to herself as she continued jogging.

"Well met, fair damsel. 'Tis been far too long since you've shared my poor wood."

The shadowy figure slipped off the rock on which he was perched and into an elegant bow. Sarah almost fell as she stumbled to a stop.

"Robin, is that you? Is that really you?"

"Indeed my fair princess. 'Tis your one true love come a-calling yet again."

The crack of palm striking face echoed around the clearing.

"How dare you! You've been gone for six months and then you waltz back into my life as if nothing has changed. How dare ..."

Robin grabbed Sarah and pulled her heaving body to him. His lips ground down on hers red lips, muffling her strident complaint. Sarah's back was rigid at first, her spine straight but soon she found her body melting into his as he began to work his magic on her lips. When she felt his tongue fighting for entrance against her teeth, she gave up and hugged him to her breast.

"Thou knowest that my time is not mine own. And that my time is not always thine."

"Oh shut up and kiss me again. We can talk about your habit of running off at the first sign of commitment later."

Sarah felt his lips crush down on hers once more and she opened her lips to his. This time, it was Sarah whose tongue sought out his tongue. She barely felt Robin's hands as they began to travel over her back and up her sides. Robin ran his hands down her back from her shoulder blades to grab her firm, round ass cheeks.

Story 5 Chasing Fae Romance

He crushed her against his hot body. Sarah could feel her nipples poking into his chest. She could feel his hot cock as it swelled against her crotch.

"Someone's happy to see me, I can tell."

Robin's deep chuckle echoed up from his chest through the hard nobs of her nipples and left her mouth tingling with the intensity. She didn't know how but suddenly she lay on her back on a pile of soft leaves.

"Someone will see us," she began until she realized that she didn't care.

"Nay, my friends will shield thy modesty."

"You know the groundskeepers are going to get mad at you covering up their well-cared for sitting area with leaves and new trees."

"Let them, I cared for these lands long before they did."

Sarah's chuckle morphed into a deep sigh as Robin buried his mouth in her neck. His tongue lathed along that sensitive spot at the base of her jaw below her ear and then cut a wet path along her neck to her collarbone. He kissed her neck while one hand began to insinuate its way under her top. Sarah could already feel her juices begin to flow, mixing with the sweat and lubricating her pussy as her lips rubbed against each other. With a moan, Sarah grabbed her crop top and ripped it off over her head.

Sarah felt her nipples harden into tight little nobs as the cold air hit them. She sighed as Robin grabbed the round melons and then buried his face between them. The feel of his tongue and mouth was heavenly as he devoured the salty taste of her skin. Sarah's eyes closed as Robin began to run his hands over and around and across her chest, his hands playing with the roundness, then flicking the hard nobs. Robin began to alternate tugs on the hard spears of flesh and sucking kisses in apology.

"Oh shit, keep doing that," Sarah cried as Robin sucked fully a third of her breast into his hot, wet mouth while his other hand crushed her other nipple. His tongue fought a battle with the nipple, driving it against his teeth then licking the sharp pain away in alternating waves of pleasure and pain.

Robin ran his hand lightly over and around her nipple, barely touching the hard nob that seemed to crawl upwards towards his touch. Sarah could feel the moan starting between her legs and crawling up her stomach muscles, through her chest and vibrating her throat. It felt like a beam of light pushing out through her mouth and rushing into the sky.

Sarah ran her hands over Robin's bare back and up to his head to crush him against her bare breast. She couldn't remember him taking off his shirt. But right now, she didn't much care. The feel of his bare skin against her own felt so good that it was all she could do to focus on the feel of his lips on her breast.

Robin ran his hands over her ribs, cupping them in his hot hands. He ran his thumbs over the soft sensitive skin of her belly and the soft swell of her hips. Sarah could feel the heat of him and the cool of the air against her groin and hips. Somehow, Robin had gotten her out of her running shorts. How didn't matter. All that mattered was the wetness she felt pouring from between the lips of her soft pussy and the feel of the clenching muscles of her groin. His long, thick shaft burned against the bare skin of her shaved mound. She could feel its hardness pushing against her. She could feel his balls trying to squeeze into the moist channel between her legs.

The feel of Robin's lips softly kissing down over her ribs and then over her soft belly was almost anti-climactic. An interlude between the rolling drums of his initial kisses and the driving violins of what was to come. The feel of his hard prick as it slid down her leg promised a crescendo yet to come.

Robin's tongue played for a moment over and around and in the valley in her belly. Her groin pitched and rolled in time to the beat of his tongue. But just for a moment. The tickling was too intense and Robin was too sensitive to her needs to waste time with such play. His tongue laved over the swell of her belly and down into the sensitive valley below. He ran his tongue from the top of one hip to the top of the other and then down along the line of her thigh. The soft skin of her mound quivered as he hunted over it seeking the line on the other side of the 'V'. Sarah almost screamed as he ran his tongue up the line there to the top of her hip, away from the crevasse that bleated its need. Away from the

Story 5 Chasing Fae Romance

river of need that bubbled between her lips and puddled beneath her ass.

The long lick from her hip and over her mound caused Sarah's hips to grind upward trying to force Robin's mouth to the burning below. But it wasn't in Robin's nature to be so direct. Robin ran a series of nibbling kisses down one of her lips then back up the other. Sarah did scream when he finally ran his tongue down the crack of her pussy. She ground her groin upwards, hungrily seeking an even more intimate contact. With a deep chuckle, Robin accommodated her by driving his tongue deep into the weeping channel.

One long lick from ass to clit had Sarah moaning and heaving her head from side to side. A quick suck on her clitoris was soon followed by a long, deep thrust of Robin's tongue lower down. Robin sucked one of her inner lips deep into his mouth. Sarah moaned as she felt his tongue fight with the sensitive flap. It felt like he was sucking her insides up through her lips and down his throat. She groaned in her wanting.

"Fuck me. Fuck me, now"

In reply, Robin chuckled and stuck his tongue deep into her. He too was ready, but she could be pushed just a touch further. Driven higher until her climax left her drained and quivering. He licked the ridges inside her cunt and then rolled his tongue into a long, hot tube. Soon his tongue began the ancient dance in and out of the gushing cavern. He could feel her thighs tense and her groin beginning to spasm. His every instinct cried out to bring her to completion but with a groan, he quit his pleasant task. If he wanted her to explode around his cock, he had to stop now.

Sarah barely realized that Robin was kissing her, forcing his tongue deep in her throat. All she could feel was the heat of his hard, throbbing cock as it forced its way deep into her body. She could feel the first spasms as the hard pipe slid over her swollen lips. She moaned as the long, hard cock drove deep against her womb. He stilled then, leaving his cock inside throbbing and quivering against the walls of her vagina. Sarah could feel the tears rising in her eyes at the frustration of feeling the fullness between her legs without the stimulation of movement. She could feel her cunt crawling along the hard sausage that distended her channel dragging it further into the hot cavern. Just as she was about to scream at him, Robin began to pull his hard, thick cock out again leaving an emptiness in her gut. He held the head at the very edge of her cavern, teasing her with its closeness. But not for long. His own desire drove his cock deep into her, slowly driving the feeling of fullness back into her crotch. It was too much. Sarah felt the first spasms. It was too soon. Robin wasn't there yet. But she couldn't help herself. She felt her cunt spasm. She felt the pushing that signaled her first release. Her stomach rolled and heaved bucking out her pleasure.

And still Robin continued to pump. Slowly his hard cock drove deep within her, rocking her clit on every thrust, rubbing against the inner walls of her pussy, milking the walls of her cunt of their burning moisture. Sarah could feel her quim begin to bleat and spasm once again. Six months was too long. Her body was going to drag as much out of this experience as it could get. She felt each muscle as it tensed and then released, driving her over the top. The spasm went on much longer this time. It seemed to last forever, going on and on, dragging her awareness down between her legs. Focusing her thoughts and feelings on the hard tube driving into her body.

She could feel every movement as Robin began to pump his hips faster and faster. She could feel the heat of his skin against her mound. And the greater heat lower down and deep within her. She could feel every pounding blow against her clitoris as he drove deep in a relentless rhythm.

Sarah almost screamed as she felt Robin's teeth bite down on her trapezoids. That was going to leave a mark, but frankly, Sarah didn't care. All she knew was that the pain drove her higher, leaving her insides heaving and clenching the hard sausage ramming into her. She did scream as she felt his teeth grip her burning, hard nipple, drawing it into the hot, wet cavern of his mouth. The flick of his tongue across the crinkled skin set her insides churning as the biggest orgasm of all built to the very edge and threatened to tumble over leaving her curled in a tiny ball beneath him.

The feel of his hot stream hitting the walls of her cunt drove her over the top once again. She felt the very walls of her cunt opening and closing as she sucked his gift of life giving sperm deep into her body. She imagined herself sucking him deep within her, swallowing his every drop, milking him until his balls were shrunken and dry. One final, massive spasm drove a scream up from her groin, through her stomach, her chest and out her throat. Her legs grabbed his hips, driving him deeper into her, clutching him, forcing him to stay within while her body rippled and flowed over his now softening cock.

Story 5 Chasing Fae Romance

***

Notes From the Author

A note from the author

I hope you enjoyed this book. I enjoy reading your mail so write me with any comments or things you'd like to see in coming books. You can send me mail at **jean.ecrivain@gmail.com** and you can follow me on Facebook at http://www.facebook.com/jean.ecrivain, or on Amazon at amazon.com/author/jeanecrivain. On Facebook you can follow my books, learn more about the characters, discover what my next book is about, when it is due, and generally shoot the breeze with me. You can also follow my individual series pages on Facebook at .

I'd love to hear from you. I won't promise to include your ideas, however, I do promise to read each and every one of your emails and comments. And I promise to at least think about your ideas. And of course, compliments are always appreciated. They might even make it into print!

And speaking of comments and compliments, one of the best things you can do to show your appreciation for this or any other book, is to write a review on Amazon or wherever you bought this book. Websites like Goodreads are other places to record your opinions. By doing so, you'll help other readers to make an informed decision.

To submit a review of this book on Amazon go to http://www.amazon.com/dp/B00T5K9XT0 and select the review button or go to the review site itself at: http://www.amazon.com/review/create-review/ref=cm_cr_dp_wrt_btm%20?ie=UTF8&asin=B00T5K9XT0 .

About the Author

Jean Ecrivain lives on a private lake somewhere in Canada with her two cats, one dog, a library, a selection of adult toys, and her one 'special toy'. In early grade school, she discovered a love of reading when she fell asleep in class, pulled off the highest marks, and was rewarded with a book. The next year, she wrote a thirty page story about a horse and a girl in composition class and she has been writing ever since. Some time in her early teens she discovered boys and her writing took a decidedly different track.

She has worked many jobs from waitress to stripper, gas jockey to receptionist for an escort service. Today, she can be found either sitting at her computer thinking up new ways to express her fantasies or on the beach, in the woods, in the living room and sometimes, even in the bedroom living out those fantasies with her own 'special toy'.

Other Books by Jean Ecrivain

On Kindle:

A Taste for the Night Series
A Taste for the Night Book 1 Arrival
A Taste for the Night Book 2 Settling In

Chasing Fae Romance Series
Book 1 Well Met in Forest Light
Book 2 Well Met in Castle Light

Steamy Shorts
Steamy Shorts 1
Steamy Shorts 2
Steamy Shorts 3 (due February/March 2015)

In Print:

A Taste for the Night Series
A Taste for the Night Book 2 Settling In
(includes Bonus of Book 1)

Chasing Fae Romance Series
Book 1 Well Met in Forest Light
Book 2 Well Met in Castle Light

Steamy Shorts
Steamy Shorts 1
Steamy Shorts 2
Steamy Shorts 3 (due February/March 2015)

Samples

A Taste for the Night Book 1
Arrival

Did you enjoy this book? Then you might enjoy the A Taste for the Night series.

Follow the continuing adventures of Chantelle, Serena, and Lord Carnarvon in the full-length novel

A Taste for the Night Book 1 Arrival
and
A Taste for the Night - Book 2 Settling In

available now on Kindle and Paperback

Serena took Chantelle by the hand and led her from the lobby into a nearby room. Chantelle could see antique Turkish carpets and even to her untrained eye they looked real, and very expensive. So expensive that Chantelle's heart skipped a beat as she was led onto them. Off to the side, Chantelle could sense overstuffed wing chairs and a couch of some sort. All she could see were the legs, but that was enough to understand the wealth to be found in this sitting room. Serena guided her to stand between the fireplace and a chair upholstered in deep red velvet.

"To start with submissiveness is a spice. Too much of it and the broth is spoilt. Look up at me, girl." Serena said. Chantelle stared straight ahead as Serena put a finger under her chin and raised Chantelle's head slowly to a more normal position. Chantelle focused on her Mistress's body as her head was raised. She noted the flair of Serena's hips and the soft hang of the dress over Serena's crotch and down her thighs. Chantelle sucked air as she noticed the soft swell of Serena's tits and the bare flesh of her cleavage. Serena's hair was black and hung down in soft waves pointing at her nipples. Chantelle suddenly realized those nipples were hard points and Chantelle felt a growing softness and slipperiness between her own legs in response.

"Ah, much better. Let's start by talking about the future – your future. And the rules. We must have rules after all or what would we be but animals. Yes, the rules. For the next ten years, this will be your home. It will shelter you and guard you. It will feed you and in return, you will feed it. For the first five years, clothing is forbidden to you. If you are good, sometime during that

A Sample from A Taste for the Night Book 1: Arrival

period, you will be allowed some basic coverings whenever others are present. But mostly you will be nude. During that time, it will be my pleasure to train you. At the end of five years, another will come, I will leave, and you will take my place. So it has been for hundreds of years, and so it will be for hundreds more. For the first five years, you are the lowest of the low. Anyone can take you. Servants, guests, myself, or the Master. You will obey them all. But only the Master is to receive your full submission and then only as he wishes it. You need not bow, or kneel, or avoid their eyes. Much of what you have been taught has not been followed for over a hundred years. I shall teach you what is now expected of you. I am second only to the Master and all obey my commands in this house save our Master, Lord Carnarvon. In time, they will obey yours, but for the moment, you are their toy. Do you understand?"

"Yes, Mistress, I understand." whispered Chantelle throatily.

"Good, then let us begin by dressing you properly. We have only a few hours until Lord Carnarvon awakes. You must be ready by then. The Master will be hungry and he loves his first taste of new flesh. Take off your clothes and place them on the chair beside you. Slowly now. Nudity is exciting only when it is savored."

The squeak of the chair as a weight settled seemed to flow over Chantelle's spine. Slowly she began to undo the fastenings where the leather lace met the red choker. She remembered her training and she would do justice to this act of release. Chantelle's breasts began to heave as she felt the desire begin to flow between her legs. It was exciting to strip before this beautiful, powerful woman. In moments, the straps of leather began to peel away from her shoulders. Chantelle could feel the sudden chill as the straps fell away from her back. In the front, Chantelle carefully held the straps against her collarbone, keeping the illusion that the leather and satin still covered her breasts. When both straps had been undone and fallen away, Chantelle began to slowly lower her hands rubbing the soft black leather across the tops of her breasts. Her nipples sprang to attention, becoming hard nobs, as they were slowly uncovered. The touch of the satin backing on her nipples almost made Chantelle cry out but she held her voice just as she had been taught. Miss Stevens would have been proud; the only sound that escaped Chantelle's lips was a quick gasp. Chantelle weighed her breasts in her hand and flicked her thumbs over the tight, hard, little nipples. Each flick caused a

A Sample from A Taste for the Night Book 1: Arrival

clenching of her lower mouth and a tautness that ran from her clit up to her stomach muscles.

Chantelle's breathing caught in her throat and she dropped her breasts to grab the ends of the leather ribbons that secured her red corset. The sudden pain as her breasts bounced sent a ribbon of heat from her nipples to her clit. Chantelle's legs began to shake and she had to force her knees straight. She had practiced this many times before but the sexual tension now was much different from the practices. Chantelle could feel Serena's need and that need almost pushed her into a small orgasm.

The sudden release of pressure as Chantelle loosened the corset caused her to suck in a deep breath. Chantelle shook her blond locks in surprise. She hadn't realized that the corset had restricted her breathing that much. It seemed like the sudden influx of oxygen drove a stream of liquid from her insides. She could feel a flushing as her body loosed a stream of liquid lust from her lower lips.

Folding the corset became a meditation ritual. Chantelle took the opportunity of the break to calm her frayed nerves. If she didn't control her lust, she would come long before she could give the same pleasure to her Mistress. And that would never do. Chantelle could feel the shift as her breasts swung from bending over to place the corset in the chair. She almost cried out but instead bit her lip and slowed her breathing.

Turning back to Serena, Chantelle noticed that the white silk shift was still around her waist. The dress flowed over the cord that circled her waist and then hung down between her legs, its knotted ends banging slowly against her crotch. Chantelle began to caress her stomach, slowly massaging feeling back into the skin compressed by the corset. She ran her thumbs up and under her ribs. Her fingers flowed over the bulge of her tummy and down to the knotted cord. With a quick yank, the cord came loose and her dress flowed down her legs, to puddle about her feet.

Chantelle ran her hands down along her hipbones and across her thighs. She longed to run her hands over her lips and into the moist channel between them. But for the moment, she avoided touching the oh-so-soft skin at the junction of her legs. It was hard. The seeping moistness seemed to draw her attention and her hands. Her cunt burned and yet the outer lips were cold in the cool breathing of the house. Chantelle bit her

A Sample from A Taste for the Night Book 1: Arrival

lip and whimpered as she ran her hands over her inner thighs and up the sides of her groin. With a shudder, she stepped unsteadily out from the puddle of silk then bent down to retrieve the material from the floor. It took all of her control to focus on folding the silk into some sort of order and then place it on the chair beside herself. With a shudder and a small cry, she sank to the floor to crouch on her knees, her soft ass resting on her heels. Chantelle's head fell forward on her chest.

The scrape of the chair as Serena rose unsteadily grated on Chantelle's nerves. Chantelle could feel Serena leaning over her. She could hear Serena's uneven breathing. She could smell the heat rising from Serena. Serena's lust was a thin film coating Chantelle's tongue and burning her mouth.

"Oh, you are going to be so much fun. I could just eat you up. In fact, I think I will."

***
Follow the continuing adventures of
Chantelle in
A Taste for the Night Book 1 Arrival
and
***A Taste for the Night Book 2 Settling In
available now on Kindle and Paperback***
***

 A Taste for the Night Book 2
Settling In

Did you enjoy this book?

Follow the continuing adventures of Chantelle, Serena, and Lord Carnarvon in the full-length novel

A Taste for the Night Book 1 Arrival
and
A Taste for the Night - Book 2 Settling In

available now on Kindle and Paperback

Serena blinked. There was some sort of buzzing pushing through the fog in her brain. She yawned and stretched, feeling the warm arm of Chantelle clutching possessively at one breast. She grabbed the hand and pushed backwards into the warm softness at her back. She could feel twin pillows pushing into the skin either side of her spine. Serena smiled and cuddled closer.

But the buzzing continued, slowly gaining in volume. Serena sat up quickly finally realizing the source of the sound was the intercom on the opposite wall. She bounced out of bed and fairly flew to the door. The screens were first. Everything looked good. Only one man stood at the door, no one else in the hall. Serena put her eye to the small brass tube. Yes, it was the Master. She had practiced this ritual over and over. There were no mistakes. The switch on the intercom came next.

"Got it, my Master. Thank Heaven you're back. I'm working on the door now."

The lock was first. Heavy old-fashioned key in lock. Turn the key. Listen for the deep click of release. Remove the heavy metal lock. Put it on the shelf. Close the silk lined door on the shelf. Then hang the key below the intercom. Now check the screens again. Throw back the bolts and push on the heavy door.

Serena leapt at the figure standing in the doorway oblivious to his torn, bloody clothing. Lord Carnarvon stumbled backwards as the naked figure jumped to hang around his neck. His hands wrapped themselves around her and he buried his face in her

A Sample from A Taste for the Night Book 2: Settling In

hair. He could feel his neck grow wet from the tears of the softly sobbing bundle in his arms.

"I'm fine. We won. No one is hurt badly. We're fine. I told you we'd be fine," he mumbled into her hair.

Lord Carnarvon let Serena down when her soft form ceased to shake with her sobs. He held her at arm's length while he ran his eyes up her form, checking to make sure she was unharmed. Then he looked up guiltily to check on the nude form of Chantelle propped up on the bed. Chantelle quickly clambered out of the bed and dropped to her knees. Her head pointed downwards, eyes properly averted, hands on her thighs framing the delights between. Her soft breasts heaved, her tightening nipples drawing Lord Carnarvon's eyes.

Serena stepped back and for the first time looked at her Master. She saw his shirt, bloody and grass-stained, hanging in rags from his well-muscled chest. She saw the fresh blood smeared across his chest, and the trails of raw, red flesh where a claw had raked its way over his pectorals. She saw the bloody bite marks on his calf. Her eyes grew wide and her jaw dropped.

"Chantelle ... quickly! There's soap and cloths above the sink. Bring two of them. And a first-aid chest in the cupboard beside them. Hurry! Not hurt badly? Fuck, and damn. You look pretty bad to me. How are Thomas and Geordie? And Mrs. Cadmar?"

Serena leapt at Lord Carnarvon once again. This time she grabbed the remnants of his shirt and tore them away from him. Shaking with fear, her hands fumbled with the fastenings of his pants. It seemed to take forever, but soon Lord Carnarvon stood nude, his pants puddled around his feet, his skin covered in blood, grass, and the unidentified. Blood gleamed from several raw, painful looking wounds.

Chantelle gasped and stared at her master. Her eyes swept down his form from his eyes to his ankles, only to bounce back to stare at his groin. His soft penis curled over the hairless balls. Even his shaved groin had a raking cut on it. As she stared at the snake between his legs, it began to rise, growing harder and longer. Chantelle licked her lips and felt a moistness seeping between her legs.

"Give me one of the cloths. You take the left and I'll take the right. We need to get this blood off him

A Sample from A Taste for the Night Book 2: Settling In

so we can clean the wounds. Stop staring girl. You can suck on him later. After we've sterilized the broken skin."

Serena's voice was shrill and frightened but it was enough to break Chantelle out of her dazed staring. Chantelle tossed a wet cloth to Serena and rushed to Lord Carnarvon's side. Beginning at his shoulders, she began to rub the blood and stains from Lord Carnarvon's skin. Brown rivulets ran over his chest and down his legs to puddle around his feet. It took several trips to the small sink before they finished.

Serena tipped a bottle of disinfectant onto a large sterile pad and began to clean Lord Carnarvon's wounds. He gasped as the cold, stinging liquid hit the tender flesh. His nipples crinkled under the onslaught of sensations. The pain of the disinfectant on raw flesh and the pleasure of warm hands on sensitive flesh warred up and down his spine, mixing into a cacophony of sensations. Serena could feel his hunger grow as she worked. But for now the hunger would have to wait while she dealt with his body. Her own nipples began to crinkle and harden as his hunger had its inevitable effect on her body.

Chantelle rushed back and forth, bringing clean supplies and taking the soiled rags from Serena. Her hands shook and her soft breasts and firm ass jiggled as she rushed from man to sink to garbage and back. She couldn't understand it as the wetness between her legs grew. She knew she should focus on his care, not the steadily straightening of the sausage between his legs. She should be worried about his pain, not the way he would taste rolling on her tongue. But knowing she should concentrate on nursing and doing so were two entirely different things. She shook her head and tried unsuccessfully to direct her attention back to the important things and away from the vision of his cock pounding into her virgin cunt.

Finally, Serena was finished bandaging the worst of Lord Carnarvon's injuries. She tipped her head back and let out a deep breath she didn't know she was holding back. She motioned to Chantelle, and then dropped to her knees at Lord Carnarvon's feet. She began to lick at his hip, running her tongue along the ridge of his hipbone. The salty taste of his skin sucked at her insides and the smell of sweat, soap and alcohol crawled along her nasal passages filling her head and driving all other thoughts from her mind. She ran her nose along the soft skin of his groin, reveling in the scent and the satiny feel.

A Sample from A Taste for the Night Book 2: Settling In

Serena could sense Chantelle joining her, matching her actions. The soft feel of tiny hands gripping and flicking her nipples drove a ripple through Serena's crotch and up her stomach. Serena sucked air as the overwhelming need grabbed and pulled on her cunt drawing it up through her spine to her chest. Serena flattened her tongue and laved a trail from Lord Carnarvon's balls up along his leg and over his groin. Meeting Chantelle in the center, they fought a battle of tongue against tongue over the territory each claimed. Their heads dipped lower, matching each other in the defense of their claims on his groin. Their tongues only ceased to prick and pluck at each other when Lord Carnarvon's prick broke through between them.

Serena's red lips surrounded Lord Carnarvon's hot, stiff shaft, meeting Chantelle's over the hard sausage. She sucked the shaft from the balls up to the bulb at the tip, her red lips matched by Chantelle's own. Her tongue caressed the soft skin under the hood, causing Lord Carnarvon to moan. The taste of male was stronger here and her cunt began to weep steadily, a running stream of need. She began to lick at the soft, purple head of Lord Carnarvon's cock, alternating with Chantelle. Under the bulb while Chantelle's tongue danced over the top, then over while Chantelle sucked on the lower, their tongues danced a jig across his swollen prick. Lord Carnarvon whistled through his teeth, his legs shaking with the sensation of two talented women loving his cock.

Chantelle sat back on her haunches and puffed air into her lungs. She could feel every bounce of her generous tits and her nipples grew into tight points with the stimulation. She could feel the liquid running from her fount and down her legs to puddle beneath her. With a cry of pure lust, she dove for Lord Carnarvon's balls. She sucked one of the firm eggs deep in her mouth. Her tongue played in the soft skin, twirling and gathering it up in ridges of pleasure. Chantelle felt Serena's lips bounce against her cheek as Serena swallowed Lord Carnarvon's shaft greedily. She sucked him deep into her gullet only stopping when Chantelle's jaw blocked the way forward. Chantelle could hear Serena as she gobbled and sucked at the hard shaft inserted down her throat. Chantelle could hear Serena softly gagging as the bulb at the end of his rigid member throbbed against her uvula. Chantelle could feel Serena's jaw working to drag every possible bit of his cock deep within herself. Chantelle hummed softly to herself, feeling Lord Carnarvon's ball bounce between her tongue and palate. Her eyes turned up into her forehead and her heart pounded in time to the pulsing of his cock.

A Sample from A Taste for the Night Book 2: Settling In

Serena drew her head back, her lips tightly encircling the shaft that filled her mouth. She stopped with her mouth barely covered the purple bulb. She was rewarded with a drop of salty, sweetness at the tip of his burning cock, which her tongue greedily licked off. Her teeth gripped the bulb, scraping along its softness, as she drew her head still further back until only the very end remained. Suddenly she dived, her mouth grabbing the free ball beneath the shaft. For a moment Lord Carnarvon was driven mad with pleasure at the feel of both Serena and Chantelle sucking on the twin eggs. The feel of Serena's tongue as it licked his scrotum and then stretched out to lick along the perineum was maddening.

Chantelle grabbed the shaft above her as soon as she felt Serena quit caressing it with her mouth. Her hand slowly pumped up and down, milking the salty sweetness out of his hose. Her tongue fought with Serena's over the silky soft scrotum that she had been sucking on. But her need was too great. With a groan she attacked the shaft, swallowing it in a single gulp, forcing it down her throat until she felt it painfully bump against the walls, filling her with its hardness. Her throat hurt but it was a good hurt telling her that she belonged to this man. The pain told her that he owned her body, soul, and mind. That she was his and only his pleasure mattered. The feeling was so intense that she almost came, her cunt bubbling and spraying salty liquids down her legs. Her insides were churning with a need so strong that she began to feel ill from it. Every little breeze was torture to a body that demanded release. A body that demanded to cum.

But it wasn't her time yet. Her Master had to release his cum first spraying it deep within her. Tears ran from her eyes in frustration as her virgin cunt spasmed and rippled beneath her. Chantelle began to strip up and down, swallowing more of his cock on every bounce. Almost allowing his cock to pop from her red lips before bouncing once again along the mighty tube. Her tongue played up and down the shaft. It traced the outlines of each of the bulging veins along his cock. Her tongue loving the taste of his saltiness and the softness of his hardness. Faster and faster she drove her head up and down his manhood, chasing the flood she knew was hers.

Serena buried her nose in the soft bags of treasure between Lord Carnarvon`s legs. Her tongue ran over his scrotum where it met the skin between his legs and up along the so sensitive crease. She could feel his clenching as he fought to delay the inevitable release. She chuckled to herself. She knew him too well.

A Sample from A Taste for the Night Book 2: Settling In

Chantelle could take his blessing this time, but it would be Serena`s tongue that drove the salty jism to boil up from his balls and spray down her throat. It would be Serena that took away his control. Her tongue began to travel leaving a wet trail behind. Along the ridge between his legs first. And then beneath the balls. Around the crease and then across that so sensitive area where his cock and balls met. Serena could feel Lord Carnarvon's ass clench and his cock bounce with the intensity of sensation. Soon. So soon. He couldn't hold back much longer, she knew. Serena began to lave around his balls and across the oh-so-sensitive skin at the base of his cock. She could feel Chantelle's jaw bounce off her cheek with every downthrust.

Serena grabbed Chantelle's nipple between her thumb and forefinger and pulled hard. She twisted the hard nob and squeezed it while extending the breast as far as she could. Her timing couldn't have been better. No sooner had she clamped on Chantelle's tender nipple than Lord Carnarvon grabbed Chantelle's head and forced his cock deep into her throat. His shaft began to pump. Hot and thick his salty-sweet cum flew down Chantelle's throat. The first spray seemed to fly straight down to her stomach not touching the sides of her gullet. The second seemed to fill her gullet and the third filled Chantelle's mouth and began to overflow over her red lips and down her chin.

It was all Chantelle needed. She bubbled and screamed as her cunt clenched, expelling a stream of cum over her legs and the floor. She choked and gulped, expelling Lord Carnavon's cum out in a burst through her nose. Her body rippled and her eyes rolled up into her head with the intensity of her reaction. She grabbed the soft pillow of Serena's breast and Lord Carnarvon's leg to keep her balance. That was all that Serena needed. A bolt of pure pleasure burned from her breast to her cunt. Her own gash began to pulse sending shockwaves rippling up her body. A moan escaped her lips as the pulsing between her lips sprayed a fine mist of woman cum over the wall behind her. Serena collapsed, her muscles turned to jelly. Chantelle followed soon after, her head pillowed on the soft hip of the body below her, her body continuing to heave while ripples coursed through her from ass to shoulder.

***

Follow the continuing adventures of Chantelle in
A Taste for the Night Book 1 Arrival
and
***A Taste for the Night - Book 2 Settling In
available now on Kindle and Paperback***
***

Chasing Fae Romance Book 1 Well Met in Forest Light

Did you enjoy this book? Then you might enjoy the first book in the Chasing Fae Romance series Book 1 Well Met by Forest Light by Jean Ecrivain.

Follow the continuing adventures of Sarah, and Robin (and Tara) in the full-length novel

Well Met by Forest Light

Available now in Amazon Kindle and Paperback editions

Sarah smoothed her black silk dress with red trim over her hips. The designer dress was exquisite, cut to emphasize, and fit like a glove. What there was of the material was thin enough to show Sarah's every curve and yet was thick enough to hide the black thong and stockings that had accompanied the package. Delicate gold chains crisscrossed the dress at a few key points, holding the material together, drawing the eye, and emphasizing the fit and the bare skin beneath. Sarah could feel the smooth silk rubbing over her nipples and the chill of bare skin between, teasing the sensitive flesh with every movement. A diamond and onyx necklace set off her blonde hair against the blackness of the dress and the deep décolletage, finishing the drop-dead look. A shiver ran up her bare back.

Tara whistled at Sarah. "Wow, these dresses are amazing. And you look hot, girl. Hotness number one sure has some taste. And money."

Sarah felt her pussy flutter as she checked out Tara. Her dress was the opposite twin to Sarah's dress. Red with black trim, it framed Tara's figure like a glove, displaying her breasts to perfection, and hiding the red thong and stockings that were her only undergarments. It covered only what was necessary and hinted rather openly at what was hidden. Delicate gold chains kept the swaths of material together. An onyx and diamond pendant, opposite twin to Sarah's own, completed the look. If Sarah's own reaction was any indication, any men they met tonight were going to be cleaning the floor with their tongues. And with a bit of luck later, the best would be using those tongues elsewhere.

Sarah shuddered with undisguised lust. She could feel her pussy lips growing slick and her tummy flipping with the growing desire. Sarah shook her head

A Sample from Chasing Fae Romance Book 1: Well Met in Forest Light

to clear her thoughts of Tara, tongues, and strong male shoulders and thighs. What was wrong with her? Today had been an unending sequence of orgasms and still she wanted more. And from Tara's labored breathing and shiny eyes, Tara was ready to experience another set as well.

Sarah and Tara both jumped at the noise of the black stretch limousine pulling up to the shop. They both blushed and exchanged a guilty glance. As one, they sucked in air, forcing their breasts out, displaying their hard nipples against the silk of their dresses.

With just a minimum of fuss, they handed the flower arrangement over to the formally uniformed driver. He placed the display in the vehicle and then returned to open the door for them with a deep bow. Sarah and Tara both smiled as the silent uniformed driver opened the door to the car and helped them into the empty vehicle.

Sarah and Tara sank into the soft black leather as the vehicle floated off into the traffic. They giggled and exchanged a glance as they noticed two small packages sitting on the bar top addressed to them. With a small amount of confusion as they identified which was their own, they opened the packages to find a pair of expensive jeweled bracelets. On the packages were two identical notes that read:

"Please accept and wear this gift of apology. I had wished to collect you myself. However, I find that I am unavoidably delayed. An unacceptable lapse on my part, for which I beg your indulgence. The driver will collect you and then myself, a trip of perhaps one half hour. We can then proceed to the party. In the meantime, there is champagne in the bar. Please feel free to indulge.

– N.D."

Sarah's eyes burned into Tara's chest as she bent forward to pour two glasses of champagne. Tara's tits swung freely giving Sarah a clear view of the taut nipples and the soft white swell of Tara's firm breasts. Tara handed Sarah one of the chilled crystal goblets and then trailed her finger languidly down the channel between Sarah's own firm melons. So focused were they on each other that neither noticed the windows of the limousine darken to opaque as they drove.

A Sample from Chasing Fae Romance Book 1: Well Met in Forest Light

* * *

Neo climbed from the limousine first ignoring the proffered hand of the silent driver. His black tuxedo seemed to billow around him as he swung around to offer his hand to assist Sarah as she climbed out behind him. Sarah watched as Tara followed behind, her breasts hanging down, displaying hard pink nipples crowning the soft cushions. She knew her own body had been on similar display. Sarah looked at Neo curiously. Although he certainly hadn't looked away, neither he nor the driver seemed to be reacting to either Sarah or Tara's enticing display. Sarah could feel her own lower body flutter at the display and her pussy lips grow slick. But the cut of both men's trousers remained perfect. Even their eyes did not seem to caress Tara's charms despite the brazen display.

Sarah shook her head. Her face lit up with a smile that only she could tell was false. Years of selling customers she couldn't care less about, products she couldn't stand held her in good stead. Only her eyes might have given her away had anyone chosen to look closely. A quick glance at Tara noticed a similar look of concern flit over her friend's face.

Sarah gaped up at the great Victorian home that greeted them. Perfectly manicured lawns led to a hedge of rose bushes in full bloom beneath a long porch. Great white columns stretched up two stories along the front porch, framing the massive oak doors. The massive steps leading up to the porch balanced the balcony running the width of the house. The clapboard siding was stained a dark, Lincoln green with white facings and gingerbread. A light orange glowed from the windows and the sound of a harp trickled over the dull roar of partygoers.

Sarah took a deep breath inhaling the scent of honeysuckle, roses, and pine. The sweet assault on her nose left her slightly lightheaded. The feel of her hard nipples slipping over the silk of her dress sent a flutter of desire rippling down her spine to pool between her legs. The cool evening breeze fluttered up her dress leaving a clenching in her groin.

Neo offered an elbow to each of the friends and proceeded to ascend the stairs with a lady on each arm. The driver followed behind, his arms filled with the massive flower arrangement. The door seemed to flow open without any signal from the party. As if the individual at the door had been waiting and watching just for them.

A Sample from Chasing Fae Romance Book 1: Well Met in Forest Light

A sea of bodies, and eveningwear in every hue greeted them as they entered the massive home. Low cut gowns framed and displayed firm breasts of every description. Tuxedos emphasized strong chests and shoulders. Strains of a small jazz ensemble wove through the low roar of the crowd. The high, sweet notes of the harp at the ensemble's core picked its way through the deep rumble of conversation and the occasional high giggle or deep laugh.

Sarah watched as a pretty, young girl flitted through the crowd. She couldn't have been much over 20 and was tiny and petite. Yet, she hefted a heavy tray filled with glass goblets above her head. Her short-cropped brown hair bounced as she bobbed and weaved amongst the guests. Her black and white maid's outfit flashed between the bright colors of the crowd. Other male and female servers similarly clad, flitted amongst the guests in other areas of the massive ballroom.

Neo scooped two crystal goblets of champagne from the girl's tray and handed them to Sarah and to Tara. With a hand on the skin of their lower backs, just above the jut of their round asses, Neo guided them further into the crowd. Behind them, forgotten, the silent driver disappeared with his burden.

***
Follow the continuing adventures of
Sarah, Robin, and Tara in
Chasing Fae Romance Book 1 - Well Met In Forest Light
and
Chasing Fae Romance Book 2 - Well Met in Castle Light
available now in Kindle and Paperback editions
***

Chasing Fae Romance Book 2 Well Met in Castle Light

Did you enjoy this book? Then you might enjoy the first book in the Chasing Fae Romance series Book 2 Well Met by Castle Light by Jean Ecrivain.

Follow the continuing adventures of Sarah, and Robin (and Tara) in the full-length novel

Book 2 Well Met in Castle Light

Available now in Amazon Kindle and Paperback editions

Sarah shifted on her saddle as her horse stamped nervously on the cobblestones that lined the courtyard. She slipped her body forward and back unsuccessfully seeking a comfortable position. Her lips grimaced as she placed weight on her tender ass. She sucked air and moaned between clenched teeth as the saddle slipped between her lips over her clit.

"Why, in God's name, are we riding this morning? I'd much rather be lying in bed and doing other things than this", she whined.

"I understand thy desires, my love. But mine guests expect a Wild Hunt every morn and I must not disappoint them. And we must be present for at least one of the hunts."

"But chasing a poor little fox with horses and dogs? It's barbaric. It's hardly a fair fight. And I somehow think that it is rather unlikely that the poor creature is a pest whose population needs to be kept down. Not here, where a little magic could do the job much more effectively. You sure as hell don't need to raise a body this large to kill the poor thing. And I've yet to see a chicken in the whole country, so you can't be worried about them. About the only good thing that can be said about all this hoopla is that I get to wear a proper riding outfit and sit astride the saddle rather than that bloody sidesaddle stuff putting my leg to sleep. Even if this outfit does have rather more bare spots than I'm used to having in a riding habit."

"And a most fetching outfit it is, my love. The open shirt doth display thy bare breasts most fetchingly. The belt doth clench thy waist in a most titillating way. And the straps of thy riding trews art most cleverly placed to preserve thy modesty while leaving much bare to imagination and desire. Wouldst that I could explore the bareness afore we ride out. We shall have to find

A Sample from Chasing Fae Romance Book 2: Well Met in Castle Light

ourselves bereft of our guests before the day is done and my control is lost."

Sarah smiled to herself and shifted once again along the saddle. She could feel her pussy bleat and grow wet and slippery. A crawling sensation began between her legs and crept around her groin and ass. Her nipples formed sharp points against the linen shirt.

"But methinks thou dost mistake our prey for this day. There are no small animals in our lands; save those few we desire as guests. We would never kill them intentionally. And our borders are sealed from the young under-fae. Should one slip past our guards, they are hunted by the servants and slain. Our prey is much harder to hunt and much more enjoyable in the capture. Unless I am mistaken, they doth approach."

Sarah looked at where Robin indicated. Two young Kitsune females stumbled towards the company at the end of a long chain. They were so similar in looks that they could have been twins. Their hands were bound in front of their nude bodies by smaller chains attached to one large chain that split to end in black leather dog collars at their neck. Their identical red hair flowed between their elongated ears and down their back. Their breasts were firm and their nipples were hard, tight little buttons on white hills. Three black-tipped red furry tails swung from each round ass.

"Well, vixens, art thou both ready? Thou knowest the rules of the Wild Hunt. If thou canst avoid the huntsmen until the setting of the sun, each may choose a body slave from amongst the huntsmen for the duration of our time here. If thou art caught before the sun doth set, then thou wilt serve the huntsman or men and any hounds who art lucky enough to capture thee. Thou hast won a full half-hour of flight afore we follow. What say you?"

"We need only five minutes to leave your hunt behind. We will choose our mates regardless of the outcome. Shall I spend the remaining time with my hand between my legs? Your hounds will then have something to follow. I will still win this contest and the one to follow, my lord." The bolder of the two chimed.

"I think not, vixen. Methinks thou both doth leak enough already for e'en the most nose-dead hound or fae. Twenty minutes watching you pleasure yourselves would leave the hunt rutting the ground and unable to

A Sample from Chasing Fae Romance Book 2: Well Met in Castle Light

follow. So be off with you then. In five minutes we shall follow."

The bolder Kitsune smiled and waggled her hips. Her hands clasped the gold ring of her black leather chocker for a moment. They slipped to her breasts as the chains were removed and she flicked her thumbs over the hard nipples. One hand slowly drew down her body until she inserted a single finger between lips of her cunt. She rubbed it up and down her wet pussy and then withdrew its wet length. She ran the finger slowly up her body taking special care to circle her nipple. When she was sure she had everyone's attention, she stuck the finger between her lips and slowly sucked it dry with a smile. She stuck her tongue out and bowed to the company. With a laugh, she bounded out of the gate and dashed through the meadow beyond.

As soon as the chain was pulled from the silver buckle of her collar, the quieter Kitsune simply dropped both hands, spread her pussy lips, and flicked her fingertips over her lips and clit. Her hips bucked uncontrollably and her quick breathing set her heavy tits jiggling. She closed her eyes, sighed once, and whimpered. She threw a kiss to the crowd and then bounced out of the gate in quick pursuit of her sister.

Robin shook his head and chuckled. He looked at the astonishment on Sarah's face and his chuckles became a full-blown laugh.

"Not quite the prey thou expected, my lady love? Or the prize? All of our guests may choose to test themselves this way and enjoy the bounty. Though in truth, it is always the Kitsune that seem to be the first to volunteer. I think they are as excited by the hunt as they are by the reward. Today we hunt twin sisters. Tomorrow, we hunt a male. I understand most of the women have a bet amongst themselves as to which will find him first. Or whom he will chose to allow to capture him if one wishes to be more truthful. Our party, are not so caring. They, I am feared to say, are simply drunk on lust and longing."

"That was cruel. Making me think it was a fox we were hunting. I suppose you think you're a big man tricking me that way. Just you wait, mister comedian. You'll get yours."

Robin sidled his horse up to Sarah, reached over, and kissed her deeply. His tongue slipped between her lips and claimed her mouth, flicking over the warm, moistness it found there. Sarah sighed and bent her

A Sample from Chasing Fae Romance Book 2: Well Met in Castle Light

head back sucking him deep into her mouth. Her tongue flicked along his, teasing him to enter her further.

"I already have mine and I am yours whenever thou wish it. And the sooner we can be lost from our company the happier I shall be."

"Typical man. It's only yours when I choose to give it to you ... but this is mine whenever I want," whispered Sarah sliding her hand between his legs.

Robin groaned and curled over her hand. His hand grabbed hers and held it against his hardness. Sarah smiled at the heat and the growing hardness beneath her palm.

"Now, it is thee who art being cruel, my lady. How shall I ride like this?"

Sarah smiled and squeezed his hard rod.

"Well you'll just have to find a way to soften it, won't you? You'll have to catch me first, though. Until then, you'll just have to ride behind me and settle for the view! Just like this!"

Sarah laughed. She slid her hand along his cock one last time, and put her heels to her horse. The tall, white beast leapt forward, and out the castle gate in close pursuit of the baying hounds and their erstwhile masters.

Robin pushed his hard cock into a more comfortable position, shifting his butt on the saddle. He guided his horse out the gate. As soon as he had cleared the gate and the few stragglers, he stood up in his stirrups, gave his horse its head, and raced across the meadow in pursuit of his prey.

* * *

Sarah stood up in her stirrups and clenched her ass. She longed to massage the soreness out but that would hardly be ladylike. She grinned to herself. Last night had hardly been ladylike either. Sarah closed her eyes, and licked her lips as she remembered sucking on both Robin and the faun's cocks. The evening had ended with one last fuck with one cock in her cunt and another

A Sample from Chasing Fae Romance Book 2: Well Met in Castle Light

in her mouth. Sarah hummed as her cunt clenched over the memories.

Sarah looked over at Robin and licked her lips. He had been behind her for most of the last six hours. And for most of the time it was quite obvious he had a raging hard-on. Sarah giggled. She had spent as much of her time finding a reason to lift her ass off the saddle and shake it as she had spent chasing the fox-women. She kept finding different ways for her tits to bounce out from behind her shirt only to be pushed back into hiding with a great flurry of attention-getting sound and motion. Robin now looked like he was ready to fall on his knees and beg her for relief. But Sarah hadn't quite finished teasing him yet.

Sarah giggled evilly to herself. She shifted her hips and enjoyed the slick feeling between her cunt lips. The crotch of her trews was wet and sticky, and the bare patches along her upper thighs glistened. The leather of her saddle was stained dark brown and her pussy was clenching and twisting every time she moved.

Just then, she noticed movement in a clump of grass on the other side of the meadow. With a quick laugh at Robin, she urged her horse into a canter and rode off after the waving signal. Robin shook his head, rubbed his crotch for the fifth time that hour, and rode quickly after her flashing white form.

As Sarah neared the waving clump of grass, she noticed a small red and white form running off through the turkey frond and bluegrass. With a quick shout at Robin, she urged her horse to a fast gallop and chased after the bounding Kitsune. But within moments, the only thing Sarah could see was the occasional wag of the tall grass to indicate where the Kitsune had run. Sarah chased the will-o-the-wisp for a few minutes but soon slowed to her mount to a walk. She swiveled her head around looking unsuccessfully for any sign of the prey. Within moments, she heard the noise of baying hounds.

Sarah stopped below an old, gnarled apple tree and watched as a faun and two hounds leapt on the shy Kitsune, bringing her down in a pile of laughing, naked forms. Sarah rubbed her pussy with one hand as she watched the sexy dog pile below her.

The Kitsune twisted around and slid down the faun's body. Around her, the hounds whined and licked

A Sample from Chasing Fae Romance Book 2: Well Met in Castle Light

at any body parts they could reach. Their cocks grew hard and were soon pointing towards the ground, dripping slickness on the ground below them. The Kitsune slipped back, the silver ring of her collar slid along the faun's hard cock sending shivers up his groin. The Kitsune grabbed the faun by his hard prick and pulled him towards her open mouth. She soon had herself twisted around with her ass and tails pushed high in the air and her hands and knees on the ground. Her cheeks began to puff out as she sucked the faun deep into her throat.

One hound pushed his muzzle deep into her pussy and began to lick with long strokes of his tongue. The other two hounds began to lick and nuzzle at her breasts. The Kitsune moaned and pushed her breasts at the two hounds. One of the hounds pulled back and shook himself. He rolled over on his back, his rock hard cock sticking straight up and his paws clawing at her body. His skin began to roil and bubble, the flesh molding and folding in on itself as he changed into the form of a dark-haired male. He howled and pulled himself under the Kitsune. His mouth plastered itself to her tit and he sucked the hard nob deep into his mouth. The Kitsune howled around the hard rod in her mouth and rolled her hips, pushing her cunt tighter against the hound that licked between her legs.

The Kitsune ground her hips against the hound, forcing his tongue to lash over her clit and lips. Her hips shifted from side to side as she sought to force his tongue against just the right spots. Wet slurping sounds drifted up as the hound licked and sucked on her flesh. He seized her lips between his teeth and sucked deeply on them. The Kitsune moaned. Her hips bucked and shook. Her feet pounded a drumbeat into the soft loam.

Her hands grasped the faun's thighs and forced him even tighter against her until she buried her nose in the soft fur above his hard rod. Her moan turned into a keening wail as she sucked the faun's cock deeper into her mouth. Her throat and cheeks worked as she sucked and licked along his length. She sucked at him as if she had been starved for days and he held the sweetest desserts. The faun seized her head and fought to keep his hips from bucking uncontrollably in response. His balls bounced off her chin drawing a whimper from him on every moist impact. He threw his head back and arched his back. A groan squeezed itself from between his lips.

The hound below her ground his penis into the soft loam. His jaws began to snap at her breast. His tongue flicked out, seeking out her hard nipple and drawing it between his sharp teeth. The hound seized on

A Sample from Chasing Fae Romance Book 2: Well Met in Castle Light

the nipple and drew it out as far as he could. He shook his head causing the heavy breast to bounce against the Kitsune's other breast and the other man-dog's cheek. With a growl, the hound swallowed more of the heavy flesh. His cheeks flared as his tongue flipped over the hard brown nob and the white flesh.

Beneath her, the man-dog twisted until his body was beneath the Kitsune. His hands and mouth continued to work the breast he had seized. He squeezed and rolled the flesh in his hands. White flesh squeezed out between his fingers and slowly turned pink. His tongue flicked out and over the hard, brown tube that crowned her breast. The Kitsune's moans rang off the trees that ringed the meadow. Tears ran down her cheeks.

The man-dog rubbed his hard cock along her slit. A long slick line of pre-cum formed along her mound and over her lips. The hound behind licked along her slick cunt and over the lips. It whimpered as it licked her mound clean. The Kitsune screamed as she felt the hard rod slide between her sopping wet lips and slide into the cavern between her legs. She slid down the hard cock and forced her crotch against the hot flesh below. Her ass rippled and heaved as she sought to draw more of the heat within her.

Behind her, the hound rooted in her ass, seeking the brown hole that hid between her soft cheeks. His long, hot tongue slid within the tight hole, forcing more whimpers from the Kitsune's lips. Her hips pounded on the man-dog beneath her, driving his hard rod deeper into her burning flesh. The hound rammed his tongue deep into her ass, keeping time with the rhythm of the wet slapping beneath him. His hips began to shake. Pre-cum rained off the hard cock between his legs in great drops. He whimpered and sucked his tongue out from between the soft pillows of her arse.

The hound pulled away, shook his head, and then clambered over the heaving form of the Kitsune. His hard cock stood out from his body, the tip red and glistening. He slid it between the soft cushions of the Kitsune's arse. He gripped her cheeks, separating them and giving him a clear view of the crinkled hole below her whipping tails. His cock curved slightly as it was trapped for just a moment. However, with a slight plop the head squeezed through the tight sphincter, stretching it and then sliding through. The hound threw its head back and howled. His paws slid around the Kitsune to grab and hold her waist between his legs. His

A Sample from Chasing Fae Romance Book 2: Well Met in Castle Light

hips heaved once, twice, slowly on the inward thrust and faster on the withdrawal as if pushing against a mighty spring. The strain of holding back set the hound's thighs to quivering, and soon the thrusts matched the jackhammering of the cock pounding into the Kitsune's cunt. The Kitsune quivered between the two cocks as they pounded into her cunt and ass, pulling out in lockstep and then pounding in to squeeze her sensitive flesh between their thrusting groins.

The Kitsune pulled her head back, sucking hard all the while and then thrust hard down the faun's cock. Her tongue slid down his hard pole and her teeth slid lightly along the soft skin drawing the prepuce back over the glans and teasing the hard flesh beneath. The faun began to hump her mouth, treating her throat like a soft, wet pussy.

The Kitsune grabbed the prick of the hound at her breast. Her hand slid over the soft, wet glans and then back down the hard shaft. She clutched at the hound's balls for just a moment, including them in the package she held. She drew them up with her hand until she reached the furthest extent she could stretch them. Then she slid her hand back down the shaft. The skin of his cock grew slick and hot. Over and over, her hand slid up and down the hard rod, up and down twice, then catching the balls and stretching them with her pumping hand as far as they would go, then back down again. Repeatedly her hand flew jerking on his prick twice then jerking balls and prick. The hound moaned against the breast, his screams vibrating against her hard nipples and shaking her aching tit.

With a howl, the hound rammed his cock against the Kitsune's hand. A long spray of white cum flew from the bright red end of his hard prick. It flew over her back in spurts to land in a long trail over her back and down the side of her breast. She shivered and shook as she felt the hot gelatinous mass strike her body.

She screamed against the body of the faun. The faun arched his body. He clenched her hair tightly in his fists as his spasming cock slipped from between her lips, spraying hot cum over her face. Long strands of liquid heat sprayed upwards into her hair to trail down over her eyes, her cheeks, and her chin.

Her hips bucked and shook as her own orgasm rippled up her backbone. Behind her, the hound ground his cock further into her ass. He panted and gasped as

A Sample from Chasing Fae Romance Book 2: Well Met in Castle Light

his hips shook with the force of his own orgasm. His tongue lolled out of his open jaws and his skin rippled and shifted until he collapsed and rolled off her. Long strands of cum stretched between his now softening prick and her ass. His skin twisted as his torso turned human, and then dog, and then back to human again.

Beneath her, the man-dog grunted and rammed his groin against the Kitsune's cunt. He rode her heaving hips, trying desperately not to slip out while her hips bounced and weaved in her orgasm. His hips were raised and his body arched into a pelvic tilt lifting her knees off the ground. White trails of liquid slipped over his balls and down his stomach. His head flew back dragging her tit until the nipple popped from his mouth. He held the position, his body shaking in time to her spasms, until with a groan he collapsed, dragging her unmoving form down to splay on ground in a pile of softly heaving bodies.

***

Follow the continuing adventures of
Sarah, Robin, and Tara in
Chasing Fae Romance Book 1 - Well Met In Forest Light
and
Chasing Fae Romance Book 2 - Well Met in Castle Light
available now in Kindle and Paperback editions
***

The Steamy Shorts series

Did you enjoy this book? Then you might enjoy the other books in the Steamy Shorts series of short story collections by Jean Ecrivain.

Welcome to the world of Jean Ecrivain's erotica short stories. Covering the range of erotica sub-genres and usually set in a world of Steampunk, Science Fiction, or Fantasy in a collection of short tales on frequently taboo subjects. The stories are hot, adult erotica and often include BDSM, menage, and alternative sexual themes. Most of the stories involve strong women who take control of their own sexuality. The stories are usually about 5,000 words long (20 pages) and include a romance story as well as the hot sex and steampunk, SF, or fantasy setting.

Steamy Shorts 1

Available now in Amazon Kindle and Paperback editions

In this collection of five erotic short stories for women (and their men) are:

1. The Magnificent Vibrational Relief Machine
2. Queen Bee
3. Pirate Jenny
4. Steamy Shorts
5. A Taste for the Night

Steamy Shorts 2

Coming January 2015 in Amazon Kindle and Paperback editions

In this collection of five erotic short stories for women (and their men) are:

1. The Bonny Black Hare
2. The Sex Jin
3. Cyber Sexed
4. Sword and Sexery
5. Well Met in the Forest